VAMPIRE HUNTER D

Other Vampire Hunter D books published by
Dark Horse Books and Digital Manga Publishing

VAMPIRE HUNTER D

VOLUME 9
THE ROSE PRINCESS

Written by
HIDEYUKI KIKUCHI

Illustrations by
YOSHITAKA AMANO

English translation by
KEVIN LEAHY

Dark Horse Books®
Milwaukie

Los Angeles

VAMPIRE HUNTER D 9: THE ROSE PRINCESS

Cover art by Yoshitaka Amano

English translation by Kevin Leahy

Book design by Heidi Fainza

Published by
Dark Horse Books
a division of Dark Horse Comics
10956 SE Main Street
Milwaukie, OR 97222
darkhorse.com

Digital Manga Publishing
1487 West 178th Street, Suite 300
Gardena, CA 90248
dmpbooks.com

Library of Congress Cataloging-in-Publication Data

Kikuchi, Hideyuki, 1949-
  [D--Baraki. English]
  The rose princess / written by Hideyuki Kikuchi ; illustrated by Yoshitaka Amano ; English translation by Kevin Leahy.
      p. cm. -- (Vampire Hunter D ; v. 9)
  "Originally published in Japan in 1994 by Asahi Sonorama, Tokyo"--T.p. verso.
  ISBN 978-1-59582-109-6
  I. Amano, Yoshitaka. II. Leahy, Kevin. III. Title.
  PL832.I37D2313 2007
  895.6'36--dc22

ISBN: 978-1-59582-109-6

First Dark Horse Books Edition: November 2007

10 9 8 7 6 5 4 3 2 1

Printed in the United States of America

VAMPIRE HUNTER D

Prologue

O nce the sweet perfume began to waft through the crystal clear darkness, the villagers hurried off the cobblestone streets and hid themselves in nearby homes.

The fragrance had always been part of the history of this village. On the evening of the village's centennial celebration, the night the new female teacher arrived from the Capital, the evening when a daughter was born to the mayor, a silent night when winter's white storms blustered—each and every time, the fragrance that swept so sweetly over the road made the people avert their gaze from the castle on the outskirts of the village as the pain of eternal damnation left their eyes bloodshot.

Why did the wind have to blow through town?

People prayed in earnest for the aroma to be gone and waited expectantly for the dawn. However, the sun that rose would eventually have to set again, and night would cover the world like the wings of a crow. And every time the perfume returned, the people's suffering carved deep wrinkles in their faces, and the community's only watering hole set new sales records.

The shades were drawn on every window, leaving only the streetlights to dimly illuminate the road where the fragrance alone still lingered. It was the aroma of flowers.

As befitted an evening of this warmth-filled season, the wind seemed to request the poetry of the night.

A castle gate studded with hobnails rumbled like thunder in a sea of clouds as it closed, but before it had even started to move, the black-lacquered carriage went racing through the arched gate to the central courtyard. The wheels creaked to a halt, and the door opened.

Inside the carriage sat a girl who was scared to death. Although her ample cleavage betrayed the wild racing of her heart, her plump face had all the color of a corpse. Even when the sweet aroma and dazzling colors crushed in through the open door, the girl didn't move a muscle.

How old am I again? the girl thought. *Seventeen years and one month. Is this the end? Can't I live a little longer? And just three days ago, I was talking with my friends about going to the trade school in town. Who decided this has to happen? Who chose me?*

"Get out," said a voice like steel from beyond the door. It must've been one of those that'd been sent to get her.

At the urging of an eerie aura and a will that would brook no resistance, the girl headed toward the door. The carriage steps had already been extended. As her nostrils filled with the fragrance and her eyes were met by a brilliant wash of colors, the girl suddenly felt as if she'd been swallowed by an abyss.

"Go straight that way," a voice told her, the speaker apparently pointing directly ahead.

As the girl tottered forward, her mind was already half blank. She simply kept walking. Although she felt something prick at her cheeks and her exposed arms, it didn't bother her. When the girl finally halted, her breathing was terribly ragged, and not merely because of the distance she'd walked.

Her almost nonexistent consciousness had detected a faint figure standing directly ahead of her. It approached her like a beautiful mirage. The sight of the woman in a dress left the girl frozen with fear—but much to her own surprise, the girl also felt a vague fascination. She knew what was going to happen. When she saw that the dress was white and she hazily made out the woman's face, the girl then shut her eyes.

What would she do if the woman who'd come to suck her blood was some hideous Noble? She knew them from the masks she'd seen at village celebrations—they were monsters, mentally and physically warped.

The girl was seized by both shoulders, and a sudden chill spread through her like ice. That, and a sweet perfume. But before she noticed that the latter was actually the breath spilling from the woman, the girl lost consciousness completely.

Even as pale fangs punctured her tragically thin carotid artery she remained completely still.

As the girl's head fell back and she went limp, the woman gently laid her body down on the stone road, then turned around. When she'd taken a few silent steps, there were suddenly footfalls behind her and she detected a presence thoroughly unsuited to this place.

"You goddamned monster!"

Perhaps two seconds passed from the time the woman turned until the powerful man pounced on her. Although he weighed nearly twice as much as she did and had the momentum of his dash behind him, the woman wasn't knocked back at all. Instead, black iron went through the center of her chest and came out her back.

When the man let go of the blade, the woman finally fell back a step.

"I did it," the man—actually a kid of fifteen or sixteen—muttered like a death rattle. "I did it . . . I really did it! Nagi!"

Judging by the way he then raced over to the girl and hugged her close, his last cry must've been her name. His movements carrying both the despair of having lost a loved one and also the faintest hope, the young man shook the lifeless form.

"Get up, Nagi," he said. "I took care of the one who bit you. Now you'll be okay, right? You should be back to normal."

"Absolutely," said a voice that poured ice water down the young man's back.

He looked up. A figure in white stood quietly in the moonlight.

"However," the woman continued, "in order to destroy me, you must pierce my heart. And you were a bit wide of the mark."

The young man got goosebumps as he rose to his feet. The girl's lifeless husk was still clutched to his chest. Dead or not, he wasn't going to let her go—that was the resolve that seemed to radiate from every inch of him.

"Will you not run?" the woman asked. "If you don't, you shall end up exactly like that young lady. Although if you loved her, that may be for the best. Now—come to me," she said. "Or would you prefer that your young lady feed on you instead of me?"

Before the young man even had time to comprehend the full meaning of the woman's words, a pale arm had wrapped around his neck.

"Nagi?!"

There could be no more heartrending cry than his in the entire world.

Cradled against the young man's chest, the girl opened her eyelids.

The young man knew her eyes had always brimmed with hopes for the future. He'd seen them sparkle with the dreams of a seventeen-year-old. And he knew that it was not his face but rather that of another young man that her eyes often reflected.

But now her eyes reflected him. In shape and in color, they were no different than before. However, the normally sharp black pupils were clouded and dark; where the memories of a seventeen-year-old had been there was now a despicable vortex of hunger and lust.

"I'm so hungry," the young man heard the girl say, yet it seemed like her voice was something out of a nightmare. "You came to save me, didn't you? I'm so glad. Let me give you a kiss as thanks . . ."

"Stop, Nagi—! Don't do it!" he shouted. Pulling free of the arms she wrapped around him, the young man knocked her cold body to the road.

The girl didn't even cry out.

"My, but you are a cold-hearted paramour."

As if triggered by the woman's voice, the young man started to run. Though panic gripped him, at least part of his thought processes remained wide awake.

In one spot in the dazzling mix of colors the young man saw a glimmer of a different material. Leaping into the riot of color, he left the whole mass of flowers trembling.

It only took the young man about a minute to strap on what he found there. As he fastened the last belt around his left thigh, he heard footsteps closing on him from all four points of the compass. They didn't sound like those of the woman he'd just encountered— they had a foreboding tone. As the ground seemed to tremble beneath his feet, the young man felt his stomach tighten. The next thing he knew, he was shaking, too.

The second the wild mix of colored blossoms to his right was pushed aside, the young man kicked off the ground. A heartbeat before his airborne form was due to sink, wings opened on his back.

Just in time—and as relief swelled in the young man, he gazed into the darkness ahead of him. Nothing could've possibly felt better than to be gaining altitude like this.

He looked down. Far below him were scattered pinpricks of twinkling light.

In contrast, a heavy shadow fell across the young man's heart. He'd never be safe here now. But where could he go?

Impacts to either side of him were transmitted to the center of his back. His body dipped sharply. Clearly, his wings had been slashed.

Craning his neck, he looked up above.

Although it was pitch-black out, the crimson armor he saw there was branded into his retinas.

Don't tell me he can fly, too?!

Although the young man madly attempted to pull back on the lever he gripped, the wire that relayed the movements to his wings seemed to have been severed, and his descent didn't stop.

"Do you have any idea what you've done?" a voice called out from above him.

Was it following him down?

"Your life alone will not be enough to atone for the crime of raising your blade against our princess," the voice continued. "Look back from the hereafter and watch what results from your reckless actions!"

Suddenly, the young man felt the base of the wings tear free from his back. Without a peep, he plummeted straight down, dropping into an endless abyss.

Unable to lose consciousness as the wind howled in his ears, he found a dull band of silver growing in his field of view. It was a river that stretched like a ribbon far below him.

The Road of Stakes

I

The road was just wide enough to allow two farm vehicles—which were relatively rare in these parts—to pass each other. Going east, it led to the village of Sacri, while to the west it hit the dusty highway.

Verdant waves flowed to either side of the road. Prairies and wind.

As the high stalks of grass bowed in succession, they seemed to be passing something along. The name of the distant rulers of this world. Their lost legends. Or perhaps—the tale of the current dictator whose manor stood on the outskirts of the village. And the situation in the trio of wagons racing madly out of town. And the reason the horse-lashing farmer and everyone in his family had fear burned into their tense faces.

"Halfway left to go!" cried the farmer working the reins on the lead wagon. "If we reach the highway, they won't give chase, since that's outside their domain. Hannah, what's it look like back there?"

"The Tumaks' and Jarays' wagons are both doing well," replied his wife, who'd leaned out from where she was riding shotgun. Drawing the little boy and girl she held closer with her plump arms, she added, "At this rate, we'll be fine, dear."

"It's too early to say. We've still got half to go—this is where we brave the fires of hell. I don't know if the horses will make it or not," he said, the words coming out like a groan.

But any further comment was cut short by a shriek from the farmer's wife.

Thirty feet ahead, a horse and rider draped in crimson bounded onto the road from the high grass on the left.

The farmer didn't even manage to pull back on the reins.

In an attempt to avoid the horse and rider that seemed to be ablaze, the team of two steeds made a sudden turn to the right.

Packed with all of the family's worldly possessions, the wagon couldn't follow the animals around that sharp curve. The wooden tongue that connected the wagon to the team twisted, and the body of the wagon tilted as it did. The tongue snapped in midair, and the vehicle threw up a cloud of dust as it rolled.

Without so much as a glance back at the rumbling of the ground and the tableware that was being thrown everywhere, the horses kept galloping toward the promised land of freedom.

The Tumak and Jaray families narrowly avoided crashing their own wagons. Desperately whipping the hindquarters of the halted animals and tugging on the reins, they tried to turn back the way they'd come. It didn't look like they would even try to help their friends who still lay on the road with their toppled wagon.

"It's the Blue Knight!" Jaray's son exclaimed, his cry of despair rising to the fair sky.

The road they needed to take home was now blocked by the blue horse and rider that stood about fifteen feet from them. However, the rider's hue was not that of the pristine heavens, but rather the dark blue shade of the depths that led to the unsettling floor of the sea—the blue of freezing cold water.

With the sun still high in the sky, an air of deathly silence and immobility settled over the three families there on the stark white road.

"Where do you think you're going?" said the one in front of them—the crimson rider on a horse of the same color. The people had called his compatriot a knight, and he, too, was sheathed in armor from the top of his head to the tips of his toes. His breastplate was wide, the pauldrons and vambraces were thick as a tree trunk, and he was so tall people would have to look up at him whether he was on horseback or not. If he were to ride out onto the battlefield on his similarly armored mount, he'd be such an imposing sight it was likely the very demons of hell would recoil in horror. On his back were two pairs of crossed longswords—four blades in all. Gleaming in the sunlight, the weapons looked so large and heavy that they'd leave even a giant of a man exhausted after a single swing.

"I believe we made it quite clear that it's been decreed no one is to leave this domain," said the Blue Knight. He was such a deep, dark shade of blue that he seemed to drain the heat from the rays of the midday sun and make the light drift away in vain like soap bubbles. "Not a single soul will be allowed to flee from the village where that little bastard wounded our princess," he continued. "You should consider yourselves fortunate we didn't slaughter the whole community out of hand. But then, there's no need for any of you to concern yourselves with that business any longer. The stakes await you."

A thin sound like a note from a broken flute split the air and a short, fat old woman clutched at her chest as she fell—Mr. Jaray's elderly mother. The rest of the family consisted of Jaray and his wife, their nineteen-year-old son, a sixteen-year-old daughter, and another daughter aged twelve.

As for the Tumaks, there were six of them—the husband and wife, Mr. Tumak's mother and father, and a five-year-old son and three-year-old daughter.

No one seemed to be paying any attention to the old woman, who'd suffered a heart attack out of sheer fright. Their eyes were trained instead on death as it stood barring the way before them and behind them in the form of knights of flame and water.

Their fate was inescapable.

The two armored knights turned to the sides of the road; turned toward the fifteen-foot stakes that were driven into either side of the road at roughly three-foot intervals. Oh, they ran on endlessly, too numerous to count, and on their sharpened tips shook the stark white bones of the impaled. Apparently the stakes were quite old, and less than one in ten still had skeletal remains hanging from it. And in most cases, those were just the spine and rib cage, while the arms, legs, pelvis, and skulls lay sadly at the base of the stake as part of a fairly large mound of bones.

However, while the families stood there as if their lives had already been lost, the corpses staked to either side of them were almost completely intact, their rags dancing in the wind and the eye sockets in their skulls aimed at the road like soul-swallowing caverns in the land of the dead. They cast a deep spell of silence.

The two knights closed the gap.

"Help!" someone shouted.

A flash of crimson cut off the cry.

The grass swayed in waves. It seemed to speak of shock and destiny.

Mr. Tumak's aged father looked down at his chest. Blue steel ran right through him. Tumak's wife looked down at hers as well. The bloodstained tip of a weapon stretched from it. The weapon that'd impaled the two people as they stood back to back had to be more than eight inches long, but it wasn't the blade of a sword. It stretched more than three feet from the old man's chest before coming to a guard that was twice as big around as a man's fist. The hilt then sloped upward for another six feet before disappearing into a blue gauntlet, and it extended another three feet beyond the knight's little finger.

Though the gigantic warrior was over six and a half feet tall, how could he wield a fifteen-foot lance with such skill? Both the weapon's tip and its metallic hilt were etched with elaborate designs. Altogether, it must've weighed at least two hundred pounds, and probably more than four hundred.

The weapon bent supplely. The blue lance flexed upward, and the two victims were launched into the air like they were on springs and came right down on the stakes as if they'd been aimed. The old bones turned to powder and flew in all directions as the new victims were run through the heart.

"Although our princess instructed us to wait before meting out any additional punishments, we, the Four Knights of the Diane Rose, cannot allow this to pass. We were just beginning to get frustrated when you were good enough to try and escape. Although this is all in sport, you should provide a slight diversion."

As if driven by the Blue Knight's words, those gathered started to run. But the Red Knight was in front of them. A crimson wind gusted between the fleeing people. Still, they ran right by the sides of the Red Knight. Even though their heads had fallen off five or ten feet back, they didn't stop sprinting. Another gust of even redder wind shot up from the ground to the sky, blocking the people and knights from the rest of the road.

"Ungrateful insects. This is the price you pay for your foolish actions."

Before the knights bellowing with laughter, Jaray's wife and Tumak's son had fallen to the blood-soaked road. The pair hugged each other tightly.

"So, which of you shall I—" the Red Knight was saying when there was suddenly the shrill whir of engines approaching from the village at a frantic pace.

It sounded like more than a few.

"Looks like we have company," the Blue Knight said, gleefully rolling his head from side to side.

Less than two seconds later, gasoline-powered motorcycles with high horsepower engines arrived at the scene of the cruel butchery.

While their engines remained running, a white-haired figure hopped off the back rack of the lead bike. He was an old man with a cane.

"Mayor Torsk is my name and . . ."

The reason his voice died as he was making his introduction was because he'd just seen the grotesque corpses that littered the road.

The riders of the roughly ten motorbikes were speechless as well.

"What the hell is this?!" said the rider of the bike that'd carried the mayor, spitting the words one by one.

Although he was more than fifteen feet away, the Blue Knight must've had unnaturally keen ears, because he then looked at the rider and muttered, "A woman?"

"So what if I am?!"

Stripping off an apparently homemade cloth helmet along with her goggles, the rider was then revealed to be a beautiful young woman with a slight pinkish flush. Her hair was cut shockingly short, and her eyes were ablaze with anger.

"What the hell . . . ," she groaned once more, the words sounding crushed and lifeless as she turned the nose of her bike toward the Blue Knight.

Two steel pipes pointed forward from either side of the vehicle—four in total. If the pressurized gas in the tank to the rear were to launch the steel arrows within, they were certain to fly straight and true into the heart of the knight.

"Ah, more prey to amuse us? And this one looks to have a little fight in her," the Blue Knight replied, his mere words freezing the atmosphere again.

"Knock it off, Elena," the mayor of the village said, breaking the silence. Turning to the two butchers, he said, "I'll make no complaint about those already dead. But could you at least be so kind as to show mercy on the last two?" he pleaded in a hoarse voice as the wind stroked his profile.

The grass was singing,

> *Stop, I say, stop,*
> *For they will never spare you*

"These people disobeyed an order from our princess," said the Blue Knight. "Until the one who attempted to take her life is captured, no one whatsoever is to leave the village. Nor is anyone to enter. Anyone attempting to leave without her permission will be considered to be in league with the culprit and be promptly executed. And it is our duty to see to it her word is upheld."

"The only reason they tried to leave was because you enjoy killing everyone just for the fun of it!" Elena shouted. "That hag of yours ordered more than just that. If the guilty party hasn't been caught within ten days of her decree, ten villagers will be impaled on stakes. And every day after that, five more are to be drawn and quartered. It's only natural for some people to try and get away!"

"Only natural?"

The two knights looked at each other and laughed.

"And we could say to you and your whole village that what *we* do is only natural. Take a good look around you at this verdant land and bountiful fields of grain—just who do you think made all of this possible? Lowly humans scratching away at the untamed wilderness with rusty hoes like stupid beasts? Do you recall what it was you said to the princess back then?"

Elena gnawed her lip. Agitation swept like a wave through the group behind her—and judging from the way they were all dressed alike, she was undoubtedly part of the same group. However, Elena quickly looked up at the knight and shouted, "That was a long time ago!"

"What?" the Blue Knight growled, his lance rattling slightly in his right hand.

"Now, hold on a minute," the Red Knight interjected. "There's no point arguing all that here and now. We've disposed of those who disregarded the rules. Take those other two back with you."

Joy suffusing his countenance, the mayor stammered, "May I—may I really?"

"You may. Be quick about it."

"Very well—Come along now, you two," Torsk said, extending his arms toward the exhausted woman and child.

But neither of them said a word, and foam spilled from their lips. It wasn't the world around them that filled their eyes, but rather death itself.

"Oh, this isn't going to work. Come now, let's be quick about this," the mayor seemed to tell himself with new resolve as he advanced across the bloody road.

One more step and the two of them would be within reach—but at that instant, the wind snarled.

Even before the geysers of blood went up chasing the two heads that flew into the air, the grass was already singing,

Stop it, just stop it,
For they shall never spare you

Just as the Red Knight's blade returned to its sheath in a gust of bloody wind, the Blue Knight's lance danced out.

The fluid of life gushing so vainly from the stumps became a thousand droplets in the wind, forming a crimson curtain that slapped against the people's faces.

From behind it, the Red Knight called out, "The rules are the rules, and we make no exceptions. And now, to deal with the little monkey bitch who called our princess a hag."

Although Elena tried to aim her gas-powered launcher purely out of reflex, the dark red stain across her field of view wouldn't allow her to do so. She had to wonder which would come for her instead: the steely blade or the bloody lance? The face of the girl was stained with the hues of blood and death.

Just then, the vermilion curtain was torn in two, as if to announce the beginning of a new tale.

Even the deadly knights and their mounts averted their gaze and backed away from the wind that gusted down the road.

But the bizarre phenomenon ended quickly.

And everyone who looked up then saw it—an inky black horse and rider advancing eerily through the corpses and the stakes.

For some reason, it would've seemed a terribly appropriate image in anyone's eyes.

The teeth of skulls still impaled on the stakes chattered in the wind. The green grass bowed, and the sun—ever generous with its light—ducked behind a cloud at that very moment.

Everything else was forgotten as they gazed intently at the new arrival.

About ten feet from the Red Knight the rider came to a halt. The face below the traveler's hat was not of this world. It was unearthly in its beauty.

Even the wind died out, as if it, too, was awestruck.

"Clear the way," said the traveler.

"And just who are you?" asked the Red Knight. "This is our mistress's domain. No one may enter. Leave at once."

However, didn't the knights currently have orders to kill any intruders on the spot? What did these merciless killers sense in the young man before them?

"The village of Sacri lies ahead, doesn't it? I have business there," the young man said, not seeming the least bit hesitant. His long hair fluttered in the breeze.

"Oh, so you want to die, do you?" the Blue Knight said to him. "What's the matter, Red Knight?" he then asked his comrade. "Have this man's good looks got the better of you? If that's the case, I'll handle this."

Needless to say, he was joking. The Blue Knight knew better than anyone the skill of his crimson compatriot, as well as his cruelty and his valor.

And that was why it was only natural that he was dumbstruck when the Red Knight told him, "You're welcome to try."

"What?" the Blue Knight asked in return, but that was only after the space of two breaths had passed.

"I leave him to you. Give it a try."

The reply had certainly come from the Red Knight. And the crimson rider had even fallen back to the edge of the road.

The mayor, Elena, and the bikers all just stared, dumbstruck. One of the Four Knights of the Diane Rose was backing down— was this some sort of waking nightmare?

As if nothing at all had happened, the young man gave a kick to his mount's flanks. He advanced without a glance at the headless corpses still locked in an embrace or the mayor that stood beside them—but the Blue Knight was waiting up ahead.

II

As they watched the distance dwindle between the two figures, the mayor and the others wore strangely calm expressions. Finally, normalcy had returned to the world. Finally, the Blue Knight would fight. That was what they honestly believed. That's how unnatural it had been for the Red Knight to let the young man in black pass.

The Blue Knight adjusted his grip on his lance.

There was fifteen feet between them.

The green grass twisted plaintively, singing a song.

> *Halt, I say, halt,*
> *Or one of you shall die!*

Ten feet.

The Blue Knight's horse whinnied loudly, as if trying to repress its urge to bolt.

Dark clouds crowded the sky.

Five feet—now.

The Red Knight suddenly looked over his shoulder—out at the grassy plains. "Hold," he cried. "His honor the Black Knight is on the way."

Another figure on horseback was galloping toward them from the farthest reaches of the emerald expanse. As his name implied, the knight on the horse's back was encased in black armor. Even if the Red Knight hadn't referred to him as "his honor," the sight of him streaking through the sea of grass with thundering hoof beats and bounding onto the road certainly had all the impact of an iron spike of immeasurable weight.

The young man halted his horse, too.

Tilting his onyx helm to survey the carnage, the knight spat, "How callous. Are you idiots responsible for this?" His voice was also as heavy as iron.

"I resent that remark, sir," the Blue Knight declared.

"Silence!" the Black Knight roared like the crashing of the distant sea, and with that single word the other two stilled. "I have no objection to you killing those who flee," he went on to say. "Such is in keeping with the wishes of our princess. But you've gone and taken the lives of even the youngest of children. We are not soulless demons! Mr. Mayor, our princess is sure to make reparations for the children at a later date. See to it that no one else discards their life in such a manner again."

The old man bowed his head without saying a word.

Then the sound of hoof beats reached the ears of all present. Incredibly enough, the young man in black had continued riding on. Bold, perhaps even impudent, the move was so far from expected norms that the Blue Knight and Red Knight could only watch mutely as he went.

"Wait," the Black Knight called out.

The traveler in black kept going.

Perhaps expecting as much, the knight in the jet-black armor didn't have a mote of wrath in his voice as he said, "I would have your name."

"D."

At that point, a single ray of sunlight poked through the clouds to illuminate the young man's face. His fairly bloodless complexion was given a rosy hue—that was how beautiful he seemed.

Gasps arose from those on the road, and a murmur rumbled through them like the tide. Elena was the first to make a sound, with her compatriots following suit after.

"I'll remember that name," the Black Knight called out.

The young man who'd given his name as D rode off calmly, as if he hadn't been witness to this tragedy in broad daylight.

At some point, the knights had disappeared, too.

"We'll bring the bodies back," said Torsk. "Give me a hand with them."

Seemingly oblivious to the way the other bikers scrambled forward at the mayor's request, Elena alone kept a dumbfounded gaze turned toward town—the direction the gorgeous young man had gone. "You see that?" she asked.

Another biker who was about to walk by her stopped in his tracks and replied, "See what?"

"They didn't make a move against that guy," Elena said as if she were still dreaming. Perhaps she was. "Three of the Diane Rose knights—and they were practically cowering, and couldn't even draw on him. He might be the guy to do it. He could save us all," the girl muttered, her tightly clenched fist making her resolve abundantly clear.

Beside her, the grass whispered,

What's that you say?

The young man's visit couldn't help but cause a great sensation in the tiny village. People stopped in their tracks and stared as D rode down the street. Dazed, they continued to stare off in the same direction for a long time after he'd gone. Every single person with a scarf around their neck pressed down on it with terrible embarrassment, and then hung their head.

"I wonder which inn he'll be staying at?" women muttered, irrespective of age.

"Did you see that sword, and the look in his eye? There's nothing ordinary about him," the men said to each other.

Contrary to the women's expectations, D didn't end up registering at any of the village inns. Halting in front of a house on the outskirts of town, he got off of his horse and rapped on the door with a knocker fashioned from animal bones. The sign next to the door had the words *Mama Kipsch—Witch Doctor* burnt into it.

After a moment, an elderly woman's voice from behind the door asked, "Who is it?"

"A traveler," D replied. "Are you Mama Kipsch?"

"Just ask anyone."

"I have a message from your grandson."

In the middle of her heavily wrinkled face, her eyes opened as wide as they'd go. Then she said, "That good-for-nothing brat—I don't see how he could do this. Where is he at, anyway?"

"He passed away."

"What?!" the old woman exclaimed, her body growing stiff as a mannequin. Her blue eyes said that the young man before her was some beautiful grim reaper. "Now wait just one second," she stammered. "What do you mean by that? Tell me more."

"He was hung up on the riverbank about six miles south of your village. He told me his name as well as your own and where you lived, then asked me to tell you, 'Take care,' before he passed away. And now I've done that."

"Yup," the old woman said with a nod. By the time she'd returned to her senses, the man in the black coat was back on his horse.

"Wait just one minute. Hey!" she wheezed as she raced out the front door and grabbed hold of one of his saddlebags. "Aren't you the inhospitable one. My, but you are a looker, though." Feeling the pulse in her right hand, she added, "Look, you've gone and got me up over a hundred fifty beats per minute. I've gone through two artificial hearts already, you know. Putting in a third would probably be the death of me. If I die, it'll all be your fault," she told the traveler. "I'll haunt you till the end of your days!"

"I'm used to it."

At D's reply, Mama Kipsch looked up at him as if just coming back to reality. It seemed that while she'd been gazing at him intently, she'd even forgotten how short of breath she was.

Nodding, she said, "Is that a fact? I suppose you would be, at that. You've got an unbelievable aura. I didn't think I should've been that winded after running just a tad. But now I see you scare the hell out of me. How many people have you killed with that sword, anyway?"

"If you have no business with me, I'll be going."

"I said wait, blast it! If you're always that cold to folks, you won't meet a pretty end." Mama Kipsch then added, "Though I suppose even if you aren't cold, you still won't have a peaceful death. Wait, already! Whatever became of my grandson's remains?"

"I let them float down the river," D replied. "Those were his instructions."

"That's a lie," the old woman said, stomping her foot angrily. "Who in the world would ask someone to chuck their body in a river? For starters, if it was only six miles from here, that wouldn't have been very far to bring him back. I think you're trying to hide something."

"He said he didn't want you to see the body. By the look of it, he'd hit quite a few rocks on his way down the river. Do you want to hear the details?"

"No, spare me."

"I'll be on the edge of town," D told her. "Find me if there's anything else you want to know."

As the horse began to move, Mama Kipsch let go of it.

Once the rider had gone so far he wouldn't have seen her if he'd turned and looked, a hoarse voice said, "That's one hell of an old girl!" The amused tone issued from D's left hand, which was wrapped around the reins. "Of course, if she wasn't such a tough old bird, there's no way her grandson would've been able to do what he did, either." Chuckling, it added, "Floated him down the river, did you?"

The voice was then choked out in an anguished cry.

Although D had clenched his left hand tightly, not the least bit of that strength was conveyed to the reins.

†

Heading straight for the edge of the village, D arrived at a pile of mysterious ruins after twisting and turning down several narrow paths.

Rising from the center of a clearing covered by a wild green carpet of grass, the walls of stone and metal looked like they'd been melted by extreme heat in places, or had crumbled in others. Although the structures no longer retained their original shapes, a concerted gaze would reveal the remains of stonework foundations, paved corridors, and the partitions that had delineated each individual room. Amid grass and white flowers that swayed in the breeze, the remains were more than six hundred feet in diameter, spreading in a way that perfectly illustrated the vain nature of mortal existence and the callousness of the winds of time.

Passing through what little remained of the bronze gates and stone pillars, D entered the ruins. The wind snarled above him. Perhaps due to the legacy of some ancient architectural technique, the wind blew through the gate and took on a strangely morose whistle before it blustered against the traveler in black.

Tethering his cyborg horse to a wooden pole that looked to have been part of a fence and then taking the saddle and bags from it, D gazed off to the west.

Green hills rolled on and on like something out of a painting. At the summit of the one farthest back there towered a solemn castle. This region could almost be considered mountainous, and while the Nobility's manors in such places had mostly doubled as fortresses, this was an exception. It had been constructed with a grace and refinement befitting the character of those who lived by night. Surely it had to be the castle of the "princess" the murderous knights had mentioned.

However, D returned his eyes to the ruins without any particular emotion, then began to walk around the barely extant roof and ramparts with a measured gait that made it seem like he was performing some sort of inspection. When he'd gone halfway around the perimeter, the ostentatious roar of engines could be heard growing closer from the same path that had brought him there.

Elena and her friends had stopped their motorcycles in front of the ruins. The air carried the heavy scent of gasoline. Just as the bikers were about to enter the area, they froze in place as if they'd just taken a jolt of electricity, and then backed away as D appeared.

Even the sirens who lured captains to their doom with their lovely countenances and sweet songs would've undoubtedly fallen victim to his beauty in exactly the same way with just one glance. But far surpassing his good looks was the ghastly aura that knifed into the flesh of all who beheld him—something that gave Elena the feeling they were dealing with a fiend even more powerful than the four knights.

"I've come out here because I've got something talk over with you," the girl finally managed to say. The words caught in her throat, and her voice was terribly hoarse.

"What kind of talk would that be?"

As the young man spoke, his unearthly aura seemed to wane, and Elena let out an easy breath. A slight spell of dizziness came over her, but she was able to stand her ground. Her friends were watching. She couldn't make a fool of herself.

Coughing once, she said, "You impressed the hell out of us. So we were thinking we'd let you hook up with our outfit."

Seeing D turn his back on them, the members of the group looked at each other. There was neither turmoil nor anger on their faces. All of them had seen with their own eyes the true power of the traveler in black.

A young man straddling a bike a bit larger than the rest rose from the seat. In keeping with the size of his vehicle, he was about six and a half feet tall. "I told you he wouldn't go for it, Elena," he said. "Seriously, why would he ever join us? Any way you look at it, he's a lot tougher than we are. All we can do is try to get on his *good* side."

"I'm not about to bow and scrape to some drifter I don't know from a hole in the ground!" the girl exclaimed, vermilion rising in her cheeks. Pressing her lips into a hard, straight line, she continued, "Everyone, head on over to Grau's bar. I'm gonna stay here and hash this out."

"Hey now," the giant shot back.

"Just who's the leader here, Stahl?"

"You are. And I don't think anyone here questions that. It's just, this time—"

"This time I'm in over my head, so you thought you'd shoot your mouth off? So, I suppose you've just been watching out for me all this time, have you?"

The girl's eyes blazed with a fierce light that silenced the giant—Stahl.

"Okay," Stahl said after closing his eyes and persuading himself. Gripping the handlebars once more, he shouted, "You heard what she said, people. We're going to Grau's!"

Once she was sure the roar of their exhaust and all other signs of them had vanished, Elena glared at the ruins.

There was no sign of the traveler.

Putting one hand to the left side of her chest, the girl tried to get her breathing back under control. The weapon she had wound about her waist felt unreliable. Still, Elena sent herself into the ruins with a gait that firmly planted one step after another on the paving stones.

Although she soon found the horse, D was nowhere to be seen. The ruins covered quite a large area, and there were plenty of places to hide. Having played here since childhood, Elena knew the area like her own backyard, but finding the traveler on the first try would be difficult.

"Just you wait and see. I'll show you what you get for ignoring me!"

As she spoke, the right hand that'd rested on her hip came up, and a streak of black shot out and wrapped around one of the ruin's stone beams. A second later, Elena was swinging easily into the air.

From the top of the highest beam—some thirty feet up—she commanded a view of the whole ruins. But as much as she strained her eyes, all she could find were scant spots of green between the ruins and the ground below. Although she was supposed to be searching for D, Elena then turned her gaze to the west. Even before her eyes had focused on the manor, her lips twisted and her teeth gnashed.

Just as her anger was approaching its peak, a voice called out behind her, "Don't even think about it."

The fact that it took Elena a full second to turn in amazement showed just how angry she was.

A metallic clatter resounded from her right hand, and out of her fist spilled a long, thin chain. With a weight the size of a small stone at one end, it was this same chain that had allowed her to swing up there.

The young man of unearthly beauty who stood behind her was met by a razor-sharp gaze.

"These ruins haven't done you any harm," said D.

"Well, I'll take it out on you, then," Elena replied as she toyed with the chain in her hand. She must've had nearly fifty feet of it wrapped around her trim waist. It wasn't the sort of thing they taught girls at finishing school.

If D hadn't come out when he did, she probably would've broken some of the beams or knocked a hole in the ceiling.

"You've been a real jerk," the girl continued. "And just to clear something up—if you think we're afraid of those lousy knights, you couldn't be more wrong."

"What do you want?" asked D.

The wind fluttered the hem of his black coat. Some of its threads were loose, and the lining was visible. The edge of the garment was badly frayed.

"To do this!" the girl cried.

A whirring flash of black ripped through the wind to coil around D's arm and torso.

"Ah!" Elena gasped, but the wind devoured her cry. Stunned, she stared at the tree branch her weapon was wrapped around. D must've had it ready all along. No doubt he'd figured out earlier what kind of weapon she carried. He stood in exactly the same spot as before.

"You're good," Elena remarked.

Her second shot made a beeline for D's chest.

D turned one shoulder toward her and avoided the endlessly stretching links.

Behind him, the chain whipped around without slowing down at all, headed back in the opposite direction, and wrapped around D's neck.

"Sucker! That's like the first trick you learn to do with a weighted chain. Where are all your tricks now?" she asked. "Or were you just lucky last time?"

"Not really."

Elena looked all around despite herself—she didn't think the hoarse voice she'd just heard belonged to D.

A second later, the inky black form leapt into the air. The move was so unexpected that Elena was left without any options.

Light shot out above her head.

With a shriek, the girl extended both arms. Even given the outstanding reflexes with which she'd been blessed, the girl still found her own reaction miraculous.

Her chain stopped the steel with a *cha-chink!*

But Elena couldn't move. D held his sword with one hand. Elena, however, was using both hands. Even taking the strength difference of their respective sexes into consideration, she should've at least been able to jump out of the way. Yet she couldn't move at all, as if her body had been turned to lead.

But that wasn't entirely true, either—her hands alone continued to sink, slowly but surely.

When the edge of the chain finally touched her forehead, Elena exclaimed, "I give up!"

The way she coughed up the words, it seemed like she was spitting up blood.

III

To be completely honest, she wasn't even sure that her words were enough to save her. *He'll just cut me down here and now*—that was her strongest feeling. Somewhere in her heart, she thought it would be inevitable coming from that young man. And that was why she was left so stunned when the pressure she felt was gone so suddenly.

But the surprises didn't end there.

D had turned his gaze toward the manor as if he'd lost all interest in her, but she saw his right hand.

"Where's the sword!" the girl exclaimed.

It was at that point every inch of Elena's flesh rose with goosebumps. She'd seen a flash of steel, felt it strike her chain, and had even heard the sound of it. Although each of these had the earmarks of a fierce blow from a skilled blade, she had to wonder if it'd all been an illusion. Could it be the blow she'd barely managed to stop, and then struggled with all her might to deflect with absolutely no success, had been nothing more than a barehanded chop?

"Is there anyone in the manor aside from the four knights?"

It was only several seconds later that the girl understood that D was asking her a question. And she didn't answer until several seconds more had passed.

"I don't know. No one's been inside."

That was all she said before she hung her head. She'd realized that if D was holding his sword, she'd never be able to stop it and would inevitably be cut in two. Then, she suddenly thought of something. Looking up again with desperation on her face, she asked, "Do you want something up there? Say, could it be—you're a Vampire Hunter, aren't you?"

"Ever been outside it?" asked D.

"Sure I have. Plenty of times," Elena replied, feeling the center of her chest grow hot. In dribs and drabs, blood began to work its way through her frozen heart once more. "There are no defense systems next to the castle walls. There used to be all kinds of stuff set up in the old days, but if there're any now they'll only be on the inside."

"How about entrances?"

"Nothing but the castle gate—I was going to say, but there's one more. Again, this was a long time ago, but when some folks from the village were preparing for guerrilla warfare, they made a hole in the wall the day before. Not long ago—maybe three days back—I was out that way and it's still there. Don't worry," she added, "it's more than big enough for you to get through. So, you going up there?"

"If you don't have any business with me, go home."

"No way. Take me with you," Elena said as she felt power surging through her body.

All of her despair was banished. The young man who'd bested her like she was a mere infant was going to fight the Noble up in the manor. The mere thought of it was enough to make her body tremble with excitement.

"I've got some serious ill will toward those clowns," Elena said. "The princess, in particular. Come on, you've gotta let me help you. I take back what I said earlier. I've got no problem with you running the show."

"It takes more than ill will to destroy a Noble," D said frostily as he looked up at the sky.

Elena imagined he was calculating how long he had until sunset.

The figure in black leaned forward casually. Without a sound, he drifted down from a height of fifty feet. The way his coat spread out reminded the girl of a certain creature. It looked just like a—

As the traveler was heading for his horse, the girl called out to him, "I'm going, too!"

And with that cry Elena tightened her grip on her chain and raced after D.

Less than five minutes after leaving the ruins, Elena found herself mired in a new sense of surprise. Although her bike was supposed to be twice as fast as the average cyborg horse, she could barely keep up with the galloping rider. Since it didn't look like he was riding a custom model, the only conclusion she could draw was that it was due to his horsemanship.

When they reached the foot of the hill, D looked back at the girl and said, "Wait here."

"Not a chance," Elena replied, shaking her head. "After all, I haven't even told you where the hole is yet. I don't care how good you are, you'll still be looking for it when the sun goes down. And once that happens, much as you may hate it, the princess will be in her element. Even if that doesn't happen, the four knights still move around by day, too. You could use all the friends you can get."

Saying nothing, D rode up to the bike and leaned over. His left hand reached out and took hold of the handlebars. A second later, he let go and wheeled his horse around. He didn't lash his mount or give it the spurs; he simply rode on with the reins in his hands.

"Of all the nerve," Elena spat. But as she gave the accelerator a twist, her eyes bulged in their sockets.

Her bike wouldn't budge. Although the engine was running, the transmission wasn't functioning.

"You've gotta be kidding me!" she grumbled. "I just tuned the damn thing this morning!"

Without so much as a backward glance at Elena as she wildly wrestled with the throttle, the black pair of rider and mount swiftly disappeared in the distance.

"You're gonna pay for that, buster!" Elena shouted with all the anger in her heart.

The layout of the grounds around the manor and the traps set there were things D had committed to memory.

Mazes, quicksand, flooding areas, spear-lined pits, swarms of monstrous insects—these were not the only death traps that might prove inescapable for invaders. The electronic brains that controlled everything surely maintained their constant vigil through the day, too. And even if someone made it through all of those defenses, the four knights would be waiting for him. This wasn't the sort of place anyone who valued his life would go.

D advanced in silence.

Suddenly the scenery changed. Greenery so dark it was nearly black seemed to have been utterly rooted out, leaving the reddish brown soil exposed. Bereft of a single rock or tree or blade of grass, the tableau that stretched before him was one of relentless destruction and ruin.

Without even a moment's hesitation, D rode right through the area. Soon he heard the sound of running water growing closer. After continuing on for another five minutes, the horse and rider found their advance blocked by a powerful torrent of water.

Clear as glass, the river seemed to swerve away from the hill to its west—where the castle loomed—as it rushed along to provide water for the entire region. Further upstream—about sixty feet from the Hunter's present location—a rope bridge spanned the river. Thirty feet in the air, it stretched three times that length and ended at the base of a steep slope that led directly to the castle gate.

When he was just fifteen feet shy of the bridge, a voice that D alone heard said, "This sure is fishy." The words echoed from the vicinity of his left hand, which was wrapped around the reins.

"The brush we came through earlier, this river, the bridge—they're rigged with all kinds of traps. That's what my gut's telling me. What," the hand then exclaimed, "you've already started across it?! You just don't listen, do you?"

Yet for all the objections and dissatisfaction the voice had carried, D crossed the bridge without incident and came to a path that ran like a tunnel through rows of trees with interwoven branches. The sun was blotted out, and shadows and light began to form a vivid mosaic on the rider and his horse.

"See—it's starting already," the voice said.

At the round exit from the sheltered pathway stood a crimson horse and rider.

The air was tinged with omens of combat.

This was enemy territory—and D would be at a tremendous disadvantage. Yet the gorgeous huntsman advanced as if that was the way he'd always gone, without hesitation or fear.

The Red Knight remained just as he was, too.

An irresistible force and an immovable object—what would happen when the two of them met? Even the leaves on the branches interlacing overhead seemed to listen intently with their eyes open wide for that moment.

However, the Red Knight quickly stepped to one side.

D went right by him on the covered path as if were completely natural. He didn't even glance at his formidable opponent.

"I've come to meet you and serve as your guide," the Red Knight said in a voice like grating metal after the Hunter had gone several steps past him.

"I don't need one," D replied.

"I'm afraid I can't allow that. We've known for some time now that you would come. I have orders from the princess to meet you, but to do nothing else."

The sun was still high. Although this was the time when the Nobility should be slumbering, there were some who merely entered their coffins but remained awake.

Giving a kick to his mount's flanks, the Red Knight galloped over to D. "Regardless of your wishes," he continued, "I will serve as your guide. That is my duty to my liege."

Still facing forward, D asked, "What would you do if I came at you with my sword?"

Rarely did the Hunter pose a question like that.

"I would have no choice but to stand and be cut down. I've not been told to fight."

Those were surprising words coming from the mouth of a knight whose ferocity was unrivaled.

"Then your lady must be quite important to you."

"Correct."

"And if you were ordered to do so, could you stand by and watch as I cut down your princess and the others?" asked D.

"In that case, I would take my own life after killing you," the Red Knight replied. "However, there's no need to worry on that account." In a tone of unassailable confidence he continued, "If you think the princess could be killed by the likes of you—well, once you've met her, you'll understand."

Saying no more, he continued on for another five minutes, and the two of them came to the bottom of a wide slope. At the top of the nearly sixty-degree incline, the manor and the walls that surrounded it were visible.

"This slope is the last line of defense," said the Red Knight.

His ordinary voice was enough to make children go pale, but now it had an even stranger ring to it—that of nostalgia.

"In times past," he continued, "we came down this incline to meet our foes in battle. Forces that vastly outnumbered us have pushed in this far. However, not even the mightiest of foes ever gained the top of this slope. We formed an iron wall where wave after wave of attackers broke until the enemy eventually retreated. Though, that was all so very long ago."

His voice cut out. And when he quickly started speaking again, his tone had changed once more.

"What we did then and do now has always been prompted by the spirit of our princess, who defends this solitary outpost. In the world below, they are quick to speak of the end of the Nobility, but we recognize no such occurrence. We shall not allow such talk in the domain of our princess, for here the Nobility are still resplendent in their glory."

The crimson horse set one hoof on the steep slope. The way it climbed so easily seemed to defy the laws of gravity.

After ascending roughly a hundred fifty feet, the knight asked, "Having trouble keeping up?" But when he turned around, what he saw made his eyes go wide within his helmet.

D was less than three paces behind him.

The soil covering the slope would collapse with frightening ease—this was to prevent foes from advancing any further. Climbing it at a steady pace required equestrian skills far greater than most possessed.

As they sent black earth sliding downward, the pair finished ascending the slope and soon came to the gate. The towers that adorned all four corners of the manor, the passageways linking all of the smaller buildings, and the very manor itself all had a stately air, but those who beheld this structure were bound to get a far different impression. Thousands of cracks formed spidery webs in the towering stone walls, the spires of the towers were on the point of collapse, and the masonry was riddled with little holes that gaped like vacant eye sockets. And while the crossed antennas for harnessing both the power of the wind and the electrical energy in the air continued to turn, they only served to make the rest of this place seem dead by comparison.

These were clearly ruins.

"Open the gate!" the Red Knight bellowed. His voice was loud enough to blast away the air before his mouth and create a vacuum. "On orders from the princess, I've brought D," he added. "Open the gate!"

Before the echoes of his voice had faded, there was the sound of iron scraping iron and a black shadow dropped across them from above. Between the two of them and the gate lay a deep, bone-dry moat. The door that barred the gate was actually a drawbridge.

While such an accessory was appropriate for a fortress, it hardly suited a manor of such simple but elegant design. Two thick chains stretched from either side of the drawbridge to disappear into the castle.

After the bridge touched down with an earth-shaking thud, the pair crossed and entered the castle.

A desolate sight greeted D. They had entered the front yard of the manor.

The mounds of brush and dead leaves that had accumulated called to mind the random peaks left by eroding soil. The roof of each and every bower had collapsed, and in part of the main manor, all that remained were white pillars. When mercilessly exposed by the sunlight, the scene didn't have an iota of the grace the term "extinction" might imply, and the light only served to emphasize the lurid nature of the surroundings to a spine-chilling degree.

"Don't let any of this mislead you. This is merely its daylight form," the Red Knight told the traveler as his horse advanced toward an outbuilding that was fairly undamaged by comparison. One room that D passed through seemed to have been maintained by someone, as it still retained the luxurious gold and crystal appointments from its construction long ago.

"As you are no doubt aware, you shall have to wait until night."

And with that final remark, the Red Knight headed toward the door. He then stopped in his tracks. When he spun around, D was standing right behind him.

"Why, you . . . ," the knight groaned as the most unearthly aura blasted his face—and for the first time he realized what the gorgeous young man actually was. "Only once in the past has anyone ever angered me so," said the knight. "Are you one of those, too—a Vampire Hunter?"

"Yes, I am," said D. "Where can I find the princess and all others?"

As D asked the question, both of his arms hung idly by his sides. He didn't have a single muscle tensed, and it was truly disconcerting. This was but one reason why he was someone to be feared.

"Do you actually think I would tell *you*?" the Red Knight finally replied with a mocking laugh. "Will you cut me down? So be it. I should love to fight you. However, my princess has ordered me not to raise a hand against you even if you take your blade to me. At the very least, you will not pass this way. D, I shall see you again in the next world."

The knight stood tall in front of the door, his chest thrown out with determination. He was a veritable Cerberus guarding the entrance to Hades.

"Aren't you going to run away?" asked D.

The Red Knight roared with laughter. "I don't believe I've ever even heard that expression before."

Even if it might mean his own death, he seemed intent on watching every last movement of D's blade. But as the knight's eyes opened wide, their depths reflected a sudden flash—a flash of black.

Seeing the giant lose consciousness from a thrust into the thinnest part of his armor—the gorget around his throat—D returned his sheath and the sword it still held to his back.

"My, but he was a patient fellow," a low voice said with admiration from the Hunter's left hand.

The Red Knight didn't fall. He'd lost consciousness, yet was still standing there like a wrathful temple guardian.

"Well, that's that. Mind if I ask you a question?" said the disembodied voice. "Are you gonna knock him over, or did you have something else in mind?" The voice cackled, but its laughter ended in a muffled cry.

Clenching his left hand tightly enough to nearly break his own fingers, D kicked off the floor. The hem of his coat fluttering like wings, he soared like a mystic bird to the skylight fifteen feet above him.

Rose Manor

CHAPTER 2

I

S everal minutes later, D stepped into a hall in the manor proper. Even with the Red Knight unconscious, he still had at least three foes here. And although he had yet to see the last of the quartet, the fourth knight would be no common opponent if the skill of the others was any indication. The entranceway had been mostly intact, but the ceiling was crumbling in places, and pillars of sunlight slid down to the floor.

Needless to say, D's destination was the grave of the woman everyone referred to as "the princess." In many cases, a Noble would have a solitary grave at the edge of some garden, while it was also common to find such resting places in the basement of the main building. So it only stood to reason that the Hunter would search the manor before circling around to the gardens. Looking all around at the hall, D then proceeded to the door at the far end.

Behind him, a voice like the tinkling of a golden bell said, "I'm so glad you could come."

When D turned, his eyes were greeted by a hazy figure that glowed and shimmered. Although it was clear that it was a woman in a white dress, the flickering light seemed to be passing through some sort of polarizing prism, and the woman's face was left indiscernible.

But even before D faced her, he knew what he would find. A hologram. It was unclear if her face was obscured because she thought this image quality would suffice, or because she didn't wish to be recognized. Perhaps it also meant that the princess was unsure what to make of D.

"I'm the lady of the manor," she told him. "Call me 'Princess.'"

Anyone who'd heard the reputation of the lady of the manor from the villagers in Sacri would've been thoroughly perplexed by her voice. Although she had a tone as refined as any woman in her twenties, she talked like a little girl.

"The Black Knight tells me you didn't draw the sword from your back, but you still intimidated the Blue Knight and Red Knight. I like strong men. Be a dear and wait there a bit until I can meet you in the flesh. You can leave that room if you like, but even by day, this is a dangerous place to wander. I've had another room prepared for you further in. Go there if you like. Of course, if you're anything like I heard, I don't expect you to behave yourself at all."

"As you ordered, the Red Knight didn't draw his weapon," D told the projected image. "If I'd taken my sword to him, you'd have lost a valued retainer."

Laughing haughtily, she replied, "So, you take me for some cold-blooded villain who doesn't care a whit about the lives of my subordinates? As I just said, I think I know you. If you're the sort of man I think you are, you wouldn't cut down a defenseless person." The glowing image of the woman laughed loudly. "You can look for me, but you won't find me. And the Red Knight would die before he'd tell you anything. Walk around all you like. Soon *our* world will be here. I can hardly wait till then."

And with her final word, the light winked out of existence.

"Oh, she's good," the voice that rose from the Hunter's left hand said with obvious interest. "She may talk like a dingbat, but she knew what you really were just from what her servants told her. She's a real wolf in sheep's clothing." Chortling, the voice added, "I'm really looking forward to meeting her, too."

D didn't reply to that, but headed for the door to the back of the hall. Apparently he had no intention at all of abandoning his search.

"I thought I told you to quit that!" a voice called out from behind the Hunter, stopping him.

The light burned a faint shadow of D on the door.

"You're a bit too insistent for such a good-looking man. Women don't like you peeking into their bedrooms. Wait until night. That's when beds get put to use anyway. But if you're going to keep at this—"

Her words became a brief shriek. A small hole had opened in the chest of the glowing female form, but it immediately closed again. Her light-sculpted face turned and looked behind her.

Quickly facing D once more, she asked, "What was that?"

Apparently she couldn't even imagine that D would hurl a wooden needle at her.

Seeming to recompose herself, she added, "To give me such a fright when I'm composed of no more than electrons, you must be an incredible man. I suppose I could kill you countless times."

"You seem quite sure of yourself," D said when he turned.

"Oh, how sweet. You're finally speaking to me. I was beginning to wonder if you even had a tongue."

"Where's your grave?"

"Think I'd tell you?"

The light flickered. She'd smiled. Yet only seconds earlier she'd been chilled by D's attack.

"Well," she continued, "since you asked nicely, I'll tell you. It should be quite exciting to see if you can get the lid of my coffin open before my time arrives. There."

A beam of light shined from the tip of one glowing finger. It guided D's gaze out to the center of the ruined courtyard. But there was nothing to indicate a grave.

"Go see for yourself. I'll keep you company," she said, her tone buoyant. And knowing as she did what D was capable of, it took incredible audacity to show him her own resting place in broad daylight. However, there was a sort of innocence in the woman's voice that made it seem she was neither arrogant nor stupid.

Standing at the spot she'd indicated, D looked all around.

"You don't see at all, do you? My coffin is buried in the earth. And you'll need more than brute strength to dig it up," the light figure laughed.

Kneeling without so much as a word, D put his left hand to the ground.

"Fifteen feet, give or take," the left hand told him after a moment.

Hearing that, the light figure gasped, "Oh, my!"

D raised his left hand high. In the sudden rush of air, the woman's glowing image flickered wildly. It was as if the Hunter's left hand wasn't sucking in the air, but rather the very roar of the heavens. But did the glowing woman see the tiny mouth that'd surfaced in his palm? Did she catch the blue flame blazing deep in its throat as if fanned by the wind it consumed? Had anyone else been there to see it, they would've surely been left feeling that the Hunter's hand had swallowed the blue sky itself.

And then, after a few seconds—the sound simply stopped. The mouth had shut. Having lost its destination, the rush of air tossed D's hair and slammed into the grassy ground.

"What in the world was that?" the phantasmal woman asked, making no attempt whatsoever to hide the astonishment and childlike curiosity that tinged her voice as she leaned forward.

Once more, D brought his left hand down to the ground. His arm easily slipped into the dirt up to the elbow. Moving it to another spot, he did the same thing again. After repeating the strange action a number of times, he'd made a hole roughly three feet in diameter. If D were to get into the hole and continue what he was doing, he'd be able to burrow down fifteen feet in less than five minutes.

"You're tricky," said the glowing woman. "I didn't think you had anything like that up your sleeve. How *handy*."

"You're a regular comedienne," the hand in question spat.

"But I can't bear to see you reach my resting place so easily. I'm afraid I'm going to have to interfere. Come out, I say!" she cried in a voice as clear as crystal.

But even though the woman spoke, nothing appeared. Stillness settled once more over the desolate ruin of a garden where the sunlight shared its blessings with the Noblewoman without prejudice.

D stood up straight once more. He alone could sense something coalescing in the stillness. It had no lust for killing. In fact, it didn't seem to have any emotions at all.

"Holograms?" he said as almost a dozen figures surrounded him. Each was about twelve feet away. Warriors. And all of them were clad in lightweight metal alloy armor. With finlike blades shielding their shoulders and underarms, their armor was a style used exclusively by the Nobility in the northern Frontier. Furthermore, every one of the warriors was translucent. Although no more than black outlines could be seen through their chests and thicker parts of their faces, stone pillars and trees showed quite clearly through places like their abdomens and shins. These warriors were not flesh and blood, but were mere conglomerations of electrons.

"Behold my castle guards! Cut them and they won't die. But they can kill their opponents well enough. See for yourself."

And as the glowing figure spoke, her armored knights passed right through her and bounded for D. The two-handed great swords they swung down at the Hunter had blades of more than six feet. Originally, the weapons had been intended for use against armored chargers and tanks.

Waiting until the whining swords were just about sink into the top of his head, D drew his blade. Although he definitely bisected the knight's torso, a pale line ran through the area in question and there were two or three ripples of what seemed to be electromagnetic waves, before even that faded away.

Watching as her henchman rose effortlessly from the spot where he'd landed, the woman gave a haughty laugh and said,

"I don't care if you are a Vampire Hunter, you can't very well cut down a collection of electrons. But *they* can cut *you!*" the mocking figure said, pointing to D's feet and a white stone that had been hewn in two—the work of a blade also composed of electrons.

The hazy figures had grown clearer, for they'd just tightened the circle around him. But how was D supposed to destroy opponents he couldn't even cut?

"Whatever will you do now, Hunter?" the woman asked, throwing her head back with another haughty laugh.

"Just this!" a hoarse voice replied, but it was unclear if the words reached the princess's ears.

Getting inside the wide swath the same armored knight cut with his great sword, D made a diagonal slash through the phantom warrior from the left side of his neck to his right hip. Once again, a pale glow indicated the path of the blade through him. And the woman was laughing, just like before. But suddenly, she stopped.

Although the blue line flickered as it had before, it didn't fade, and the upper half of the warrior's body slowly slipped off the lower half. Even after the torso hit the ground, the legs remained standing. Flecks of blue light then spread from the wound, throwing a more vivid light on the scenery behind the warrior before his body broke into a millions fragments and vanished.

"Do my eyes deceive me? You really are good," the woman said, her voice tinged with excitement. What was she thinking? "Get him!" she cried. "Kill him already!"

At her command, her guards made a deadly charge, their great swords and spears glinting in the sunlight.

D met them head-on. Supposedly impervious spears were hewn in two, and swords that had met only empty space sailed through the air with both arms still attached to them. Perhaps it would've been foolish to inquire just what technique allowed the Hunter to cut through conglomerations of electrons.

In a scant three seconds, D had dispatched the phantasmal attackers. A few streaks of pale blue lightning zipped around the garden, and then peace reigned once more.

"Impressive. I've never seen anyone so incredible," the glowing figure remarked with genuine regret. "If you can cut down illusions, there's no way to stop you. I wonder if I'm as good as finished now? Of course, I do still have *other* guards," she said, turning her glowing face to the heavens.

A speck of black appeared in the blue sky, quickly separating into a few smaller parts that came drifting down around D in the space of two breaths.

One of the most fearsome phrases that'd been passed down from the distant reign of the Nobility was "the guardians from above." A prime example of those defenses had been seen in the southern Frontier, in the domain of a Noble family known as the Brockdens. Their territory covered thousands of square miles, and everything necessary for its defense came from the sky— bolts of steel-melting lightning, ground-devouring storms of acid rain, and even monstrous beasts that could chew their way through mechanical troops.

And now, D was surrounded by a pack of gigantic spiders. They were three feet high, had bodies more than six feet long, and would've measured more than thirty feet across from the end of one leg to the other with their limbs fully extended. The sight of them snipping their exposed fangs together like metallic blades while a yellow fluid dripped from their maws was chilling enough to freeze even the most vicious of beasts in horror.

Though several theories attempted to account for the sudden appearance of such creatures from the sky, the most probable of them suggested that the monsters were released from "arsenals" flying hundreds of miles above the earth. Several decades earlier, one such craft had crashed. In addition to the large-caliber particle beam cannons and weather disrupters, investigators on the scene were also amazed to find the remains of a variety of monstrosities, each covered with a simple form of heat-shielding armor and strapped to a braking rocket. The armor must have been to protect the creatures from air friction during their descent.

The six spiders bent all of their legs in unison, and darkness enveloped D. The spiders' sudden leap had hidden the sun. But this was no ordinary darkness—there wasn't a speck of light anywhere. D's vision had been taken from him in an instant.

As the glowing woman watched the black forms of the spiders raining down on the gorgeous young man, she heaved a sigh. She was sure that this was the end of him. But before she could hear meat and bones being devoured, the light returned. And different sounds rang out—those of steel severing flesh and the agonized screams that spilled from the mutilated creatures. That's what the woman heard.

When the glowing figure turned around, D was standing there. Three of the six spiders lay at his feet, while the other three had returned to their original positions and were staring now at the twitching bodies of their compatriots and the beautiful butcher.

"You've gone and done it again, haven't you?" the dumbfounded figure of light remarked. "I've had quite enough of this. I'm running out of pawns. You other three—do something about him already!"

But the woman's impassioned cry wasn't enough to move the survivors into action. It was as if the sight of the Hunter gripping a gore-soaked blade but personally unsullied by a single spot of blood had utterly robbed them of their nerve.

"Do it! You know, that thing you do!" the woman cried.

The spiders seemed to understand what she had in mind. Their black bodies began to bulge in places, giving way to conical protuberances that sent yellowish streams of fluid into the air without a sound. For all their resemblance to giant spiders, these monsters were actually something else, and what they launched was no doubt some bodily excretion.

As soon as the liquid settled like a mist on them, the marble pillars and ground all began to give off a white smoke.

"Yes! That's it!" the jubilant figure of light exclaimed, but then she gasped aloud and froze in place.

The young man in black appeared to be enveloped by the deadly yellow rain, but a split second later, he came down right in front of the woman. The spot he'd leapt to was the safest place imaginable. Although she was merely an illusion, the creatures didn't let their deadly rain fall on their mistress.

Flashes of white light sank between the eyes of the befuddled monsters, and all three of them fell forward together to lie motionless.

Watching intently as D took the remaining wooden needles in his left hand and put them back in his coat, the glowing woman paused a second before saying, "Well, it looks like there's nothing more I can do. Say, you wouldn't mind teaching me how to do that needle-throwing trick later, would you?"

Making no reply to her stupefying remark, D returned to spot where she was supposed to be buried.

When he touched his left hand to the ground, a voice exclaimed, "What's this, now?"

The dubious tone issued from the point where the hand made contact with the soil.

"This is a curious development," the hoarse tone continued. "Her grave's vanished. I wonder, has it gone up into the sky or deep into the earth?"

As D turned, his eyes were greeted by the fading figure of light.

"Under the circumstances, I had no choice but to run away, grave and all. See you. Wait until night," she said, her hues melting into the sunlight.

"Interesting gal," the hoarse voice remarked to D as the Hunter sheathed his sword. "Still, I've gotta wonder if she's worth all those knights risking their lives. Well, I suppose that's the tragedy. At any rate, let's wait until nightfall."

In lieu of an answer, D turned his gaze to a wall on the west side of the ruins. A familiar figure was pushing her bike as she cautiously approached. It was Elena.

"What, another tomboy already? Looks like we've got feisty females by the handful this time, eh?"

Naturally, there was no reply.

II

Even when the sun went down, Elena showed no sign of going home, and D didn't force the issue. Perhaps he figured he could put her to sleep if it became necessary.

When Elena had joined him again in the ruined garden, she'd groused, "You certainly had nerve leaving me back there like that." But she didn't sound particularly angry. Apparently, she wasn't stupid. When D didn't give her any response, she'd continued, "You know, I saw your fight with those spiders just now. I'm gonna stay here with you until night."

After that, she'd gone on to tell him exactly how much trouble it'd been to repair her bike, and then she fell silent.

Three hours later, the blue of the sky was deepening. Sitting on a flat piece of stone wreckage a short distance from D, Elena began to tremble slightly.

"Scared?" said D, although why he'd even bother to ask her that was anyone's guess.

"It's just excitement—getting ready to fight," Elena replied, hugging her own shoulders.

"Are you scared?" D asked her once more.

Elena continued to quake. Then she said, "Of course!" Her tone was incensed. "I'm not a Hunter. I'm just a normal person. There's not a chance in hell I wouldn't be scared of the Nobility."

"Then why did you come?"

"None of your business!" the girl snapped back, turning her head away roughly and flicking the hair out of her eyes. "As long as those bastards are here, our village will never know peace. The mayor and his advisors all have their tails between their legs. I'd like to beat the hell out of folks like that even worse than I wanna lay into the Nobility!"

"The village looks peaceful enough," said D. "And everyone seems satisfied."

Elena turned and looked back at him in astonishment. "You've already figured out what's going on here, have you?" she said in a low, twisting sort of voice. "The villagers—and I mean *everyone*—have gotten so damned used to being ruled. As long as there's Nobility in this castle, the fields stay green no matter how dry it gets, and we can harvest as much grain as we need. No matter where else you go, you'll never find a village as well off as ours. But it's all a sham. When the water dries up in summer, the regular thing to do is dig a new well with the sweat of your own brow. And in winter, it's only natural to stay up nights tending bonfires so your fields and ponds don't freeze. Raising as much food as you like whenever you want and having storehouses packed with the stuff—now *that* is crazy!" Elena said, her confession tinged with self-loathing.

"Did you notice how many folks there were with scarves wrapped around their necks?" the biker continued. "They're all victims of the Nobility. But the Noble in this castle is good at drinking blood, and she can feed on them without killing them or turning them into Nobility. And we've got Mama Kipsch going for us, too. She's a genius at witch doctoring, and she saves everyone from the wounds they're left with. Now, if it was me and a Noble had sucked my blood, I'd be ashamed to live. But no one around here's got any pride at all. Have you heard of any other village in this day and age where people just sit back and let the Nobility suck their blood?"

Saying nothing, D soaked in the moonlight.

Realizing that the sight of the young man made her mind wander, Elena hurriedly turned her thoughts to something else. "Those bastards—," she started to say, but her eyes suddenly narrowed. Sniffing once or twice, she said, "What's that smell?"

"Roses," D replied.

The blue darkness was shifting toward pitch black. As if to praise the coming world, the faint aroma of flowers had started to mix with air that still held the last lustrous remnants of daylight.

"Ah!" she gasped with new surprise.

All around her—actually, around both of them—little glowing points of whiteness came to life. And the glow wasn't that of any light. It was from flowers. Where had they been hiding?

In the murkiness, white rosebuds had begun to open their petals in splendor. What's more, the glow came from within the flowers themselves. These nocturnal roses gave off a light of their own.

Elena closed her eyes—she thought this wasn't possible. How could flowers this beautiful bloom in such a fearful place? She simply couldn't believe it. And she didn't want to see them. The demon's lair was supposed to be more vile than this, and yet sharp lights shone in the darkness. The roses had burned their image into her retinas. Elena feared the way they tried to make her feel.

She opened her eyelids once more.

A dazzling display of life had begun to cover the garden. Resplendently blossoming white roses appeared, and all around them, elegant spirals of color continued to bloom in pale purple, crimson, blue, and even black. This symphony of brilliant lights left Elena in a motionless daze. Before she knew it the hour would grow later and later, and the people of the night would awaken and quickly find her there—

However, a powerful hand caught hold of her shoulder and a hoarse voice rang in her ear, saying, "Here it comes, missy."

As something that felt like ice water raced from her shoulder to her brain, Elena returned to her senses. She quickly turned her head.

Three figures suddenly stood in the hall of the main building.

"So good of you to come," said the knight in blue armor. "Mere words cannot convey your boldness, as you come here of your own accord after seeing us, and you even threaten the very resting place of our princess. However, you'll never leave here alive."

"Or would you care to become one of us?" the Red Knight inquired in a low voice. His tone wasn't quite as forceful as that of the Blue Knight, but it was understandable given the fact he'd been knocked out earlier by D. "With your skill, you deserve to stand shoulder to shoulder with us. But if that doesn't suit your fancy, we can destroy both you and the girl."

"You said there were four knights," D replied quietly. His aura was so eerie that it seemed for a second as if the sweet perfume had left the air. "Blue, Red, Black—you still seem to be a color short."

"And you may count yourself fortunate in that regard," said the Blue Knight. His two compatriots did nothing to indicate their agreement. Apparently, the fourth knight was someone who was not to be mentioned lightly.

"On the Frontier, there is but a thin line between life and death," said the Black Knight, who until now had remained silent. His voice was a monotone. "As a Hunter, I'm sure you appreciate that. And now that you've entered our castle, we have no choice but to fight until you, or we, are dead. However, it would be a pity to have to take a life like yours. I won't ask that you ride with us. But at the very least, could you swear fealty to our princess?"

"Okay, stop trying to make us laugh already!" Elena exclaimed. Until a few minutes ago, her body had trembled, but now it shook in a new way—with rage. "This man is a gift from God, a huntsman sent here to slay you all. Why the hell would he ever want to serve that monster?! Just watch. We don't need any help from those gutless worms in my village. Him and me will put an end to all of you!"

The three knights fell silent, but it wasn't that they were amazed by the girl's fighting words.

Having finished speaking, Elena suddenly found herself breathless. It was just such a silence.

"You called our princess a monster, didn't you?" said the Blue Knight.

"Those words shall cost you!" the Red Knight declared.

Seeming somewhat more personable than the other two, the Black Knight muttered, "Does their idiocy know no bounds?"

"What is it we've done that's so terrible? Haven't you been given a life of peace and plenitude?" asked the Blue Knight

"And how many people have been killed in return?!"

"You can't get something for nothing. It's a fair price."

"A life of peace in exchange for the lives of our friends? Spare me! The others may be able to stomach that, but not me. I spit on your deal, and will till the day I die."

"In that case, your spitting days will shortly be at an end," the Blue Knight jeered as he jumped down to the ground.

At the same time, smoke and blue flames poured from the motorcycle's exhaust pipes. The ancient garden was shaken by an engine roar that hardly suited such a place. Elena meant business.

"Insulting our princess is a grave crime. Your death won't be an easy one." To D, he added, "Stay out of this, Hunter."

"You took the words right out of my mouth!" Elena said, kicking firmly off the ground and sliding to one side. The wheels of her bike could be turned a full three-hundred-sixty degrees. "Even without his help, I can still take out the likes of you one-on-one. I'll show you what a human's capable of, you monster flunky!"

"That does it!" the Blue Knight exclaimed, the brief phrase seething with anger. Lowering the lance in his right hand, the Noble's knight was a daunting sight as he took a purposeful step forward.

Elena rolled back a pace on her bike. And stiff though it seemed, she definitely had a smile on her lips—the girl certainly had nerve to spare.

D didn't move. He wasn't there to keep the other two knights from interfering. Rather, he'd become another observer of Elena's deadly conflict. Everyone understood the rules.

"I shall bring the battle to you," said the Blue Knight.

"Come and get it!"

The instant Elena shouted that, she angled her exhaust pipes toward the ground and shifted her bike out of its current acceleration mode to activate its boosters. Nozzles wailing all the while, the bike carried Elena straight to the left.

The blue figure was still in the same spot, his lance unraised.

I've got him baffled, Elena thought as she felt an explosion of delight. Her right thumb pressed the firing button.

Go! An ember hit the tails of the rockets in the launch tubes mounted on either side of the girl's bike. Shooting sparks all the while, a trio of three-foot-long implements of death streaked at the Blue Knight.

Not moving from his spot, he merely rotated his blue wrist a bit. The Blue Knight's whole body grew hazy, and at that instant, the three missiles were easily deflected right in front of him. A mere twist of his wrist was enough to keep his lance spinning like a windmill. And that was only the beginning—the knight's superhuman skill made the tapered projectiles shoot up for an instant, then sent them speeding back at Elena retracing the very same path they'd followed to him.

The girl straddling the bike had no way to escape them.

But just then, it seemed as if the roar of her engine threw the missiles into disarray. The trio of murderous projectiles hit the ground some forty feet from her at an acute angle, and then fell over as if their own weight hadn't driven them in deep enough.

"Fancy that," the Blue Knight muttered.

About six feet from her original location, Elena sat on her bike grinning.

It was difficult to believe a machine and a mere slip of a girl were capable of a feat of such ungodly speed. As she'd slipped to one side, the Blue Knight's eyes hadn't even seen her change position.

"You've got some tricky moves, don't you? But you've had it now!" Elena cried. Her finger slid across the bike's gauges, and its headlight disgorged a beam of crimson. Roughly a year earlier, she'd acquired this laser emitter during a shopping expedition in the northern Frontier. Although originally intended for communications, at distances of fifteen hundred feet or less it was more than capable of maiming or killing.

A crimson flower bloomed on the left half of the Blue Knight's chest. In a matter of seconds, however, it lost its color and the armor returned to its original hue.

"Too bad," said the Blue Knight, his lance whistling in his right hand. He wouldn't allow his prey to escape a second blow.

Elena smirked at him. "The game's just getting started!"

"And whatever could you—," the Blue Knight began to say, but the rest of the sentence was lost. As he took a step forward, a beam of light struck his face.

Though the knight didn't cry out, he shielded his eyes and backed away. As he came to a halt, Elena and her bike flew at him and knocked his blue-armored form to the ground.

"Now for the coup de grace," Elena said, raising her right hand. The sharpened tip of the steel pipe she held was aimed right at the Blue Knight's heart.

A flash of light raced toward the end of the weapon. The electric shock not only knocked the pipe from Elena's hand, but also left her whole body numb.

"Knocked on your behind by a woman? Let that be a lesson to you," the Black Knight said gravely. Blue light spilled from the tip of the finger he'd extended. Electrical discharge.

"Goddamn . . . cheaters . . . ," Elena groaned.

It was amazing that she didn't fall off the bike or topple over with it. And for all her agonized panting, the gleam in her eyes declared that the fight would go on.

"You needn't have interfered like that," the Blue Knight said as he got to his feet.

Elena wasn't scared. Revving her bike with her numbed hand, she endeavored to maintain her battle-readiness. She was definitely tenacious.

"Well played, missy. You can tell them in heaven that you earned the praise of the Blue Knight."

The knights watched with satisfaction as their compatriot hauled back mightily with his lance and launched it at Elena's chest in a gleaming blur.

With a mellifluous sound, the lance jolted upward. And then it completely reversed direction and headed back at the chest of the Blue Knight. Naturally, the knight was able to catch it in his bare hands, though the effort staggered him and he was once more knocked back on his ass.

The three knights gazed in rapture at the powerful figure in a black coat who stood before Elena. Was their reaction a pure response to the young man's good looks, or was it the joy they felt as warriors at the prospect of doing battle with such a man?

"Are you determined to do this?" the Red Knight asked in a weary tone. "We should've known you could never live under the same roof as us. Before the princess awakens, we shall take matters into our own hands."

Not only the air, but even the flowers blooming so grandly seemed to freeze.

The three knights spread out without making a sound.

Against them stood D, alone. Basking in the moonlight, with the blade that'd deflected the lance in one hand, he was adorned with roses of blue, red, black, and white. The sight of him not only left his three opponents spellbound, but also captivated the agonized Elena.

The Red Knight had all his weight balanced on the tip of his foot. One way or another, life and death were clearly a heartbeat away from colliding in a shower of sparks.

And at just that moment, a voice as distinct as a rose flowed out into the still night it suited so well, crying, "Hold!"

A Wish Cloaked in Darkness

CHAPTER 3

I

The reaction of the three knights was almost comical to see. At the sound of the chiming voice, each had fallen to one knee right where he was. Since the voice had come from behind the trio, only D and Elena could actually see the speaker. As the girl remained slumped against her bike's handlebars, a gasp of surprise slipped from her.

Moonlight rained down on the woman, melting into her white dress when it struck the shoulders, the bust, the skirt. For an instant, each spot glistened like a collection of tiny jewels, but this sight couldn't be enjoyed for more than a heartbeat before ripples spread across the surface of the dress and the gleam faded away. Her brow and eyes, nose and lips—each beautiful part had been so delicately arranged they would leave any poet incapable of ever setting his pen down again. With her crystal-clear gaze trained on D all the while, the young lady brought the rose she held up to her mouth. Her lips were so red that it seemed they'd stain the petals.

"So we finally meet in my world, D and whoever-you-are," she said.

The moonlight gave a pearly luster to the lips of the woman—although given her youthful visage, it would've been more accurate to call her a girl. It was night now.

"Since you've taken all the trouble to come up here, would you join me for a spot of tea? If you don't mind the company, that is."

"Princess!" both the Red Knight and Blue Knight cried.

"Silence!" the princess snapped at them as if they were a pair of high-spirited children. The rose whipped around, painting a streak of white in the air. "The prospect of that filthy moppet coming along doesn't thrill me, but I'm sure you won't agree to anything unless she can accompany you. Both of you, follow me," she said as if she were giving orders to her retainers, rolling the flower between her fingertips all the while. But the young lady stopped immediately. Her expression tightened, but she quickly formed a smile and said, "Don't be that way. Are you all business? You may be eminently trusting, but I'm sure you're equally stubborn." Here the young woman tilted her head a bit to one side. "Say, I have an idea. Would you join me in a little competition?"

It was not D, but rather the trio of knights who froze where they were. Still, it was remarkable how the warriors never took their eyes off of the Hunter for a second.

"Oh," she laughed, "you should be accustomed to my whims by now. Don't make such a scene in front of your foe. You know, I said a little competition, but I'm loath to engage in anything as unseemly as a drawn-out sword fight. Let's do something light and refreshing. I'll stand right in front of you, and you come at me any way you wish. But only once," she said. "If you cut me, I lose. And if by some chance I'm unscathed, you lose. In which case the two of you will have to join me for tea. What do you think?"

Everyone's eyes were riveted to D. Oddly enough, the look the three knights gave him didn't carry as much anger or menace as it did a powerful tinge of dependence—and that included the eyes of the Black Knight.

"Let's do it," said D.

The princess, incredibly enough, snapped her fingers. "Fantastic! I just adore decisive men."

Her body seemed to float through the air, and she came to stand before D with just the faintest ruffling of the hem of her dress.

"Princess!" the Blue Knight shouted as he prepared to dash to her aid.

"I believe I told you to be silent, didn't I?" she said, her voice flying like a spear of ice to nail her guardian in blue firmly in place. "There will be no interruptions now," the princess told the Hunter. "So, shall we get started?" she asked, her tone incredibly innocent even as she invited a blow from his blade.

While she was a full-grown woman and a beautiful one at that, the gap between the way she looked and the way she sounded wasn't so much strange as it was bewitching, and even another female like Elena found herself swallowing hard. When faced with such charm, a Hunter of even the firmest resolve would've found himself suddenly unable to attack her, stripped of not only malice but of all hostility. Anyone but D, that is.

A flash of white light came straight down at the top of the princess's head—a merciless blow from D's sword. However, Elena forgot all about the numbness that had spread through her entire body.

The enchanting princess had clearly been split in two from the crown of her head to her crotch, but she was smiling.

"Which of us won?" she asked. But who would've imagined anyone who'd felt the edge of D's sword would live to frame such a question? The princess was twirling the white rose right in front of her nose.

"You did," D said, sheathing his blade without another word.

"Oh, I'm so glad you've put your sword away. I take it you trust me when I say those three won't lay a hand on you. I like you better with each passing minute. And I have some really delicious tea to offer you."

The Hunter and the biker followed the princess through a doorway into the main building. The knights didn't come with them, for the princess had ordered them to remain there. What's more, she'd told them they weren't to do anything to the girl's motorcycle, and the trio acquiesced.

The interior of the manor had every imaginable luxury. Seeing how generous the Nobility had been in their use of crystal and gemstones, gold and the legendary precious metals their kind had synthesized, Elena could only stare in amazement. Her paralysis passed when D's left hand touched her.

"Unbelievable . . . So this is what Nobles' houses look like?" she muttered in amazement as they passed the base of a crystal statue that looked to be over sixty feet tall. She meant every word.

Fog coursed around the three of them incessantly, and as it writhed around their bodies, it took the shape of gorgeous men and women. When Elena waved her hand through them, they faded away, leaving only a smile that wasn't really a smile.

"As you can see, nothing has changed in my manor. By day, it may not be much to look at, but it returns to its glory when my time comes. Like it?" the princess inquired innocently.

D replied, "The Nobility dreamed of the daytime. Do they dream of the nights now, too?"

"Dear me, that's a terrible thing to say! I'll have you know I'm as alive as can be. No different from yourself, my good dhampir."

Elena thought her heart was about to fly out of her mouth.

"Oh, does that surprise you, child? You've known him even longer than I have—how could you not notice? I guess you humans really are terribly stupid after all, aren't you?"

"How do you know that's what he is?" Elena asked, having worked up her courage once more. The fear the Nobility inspired in humans was overwhelming both mentally and emotionally. Her voice was hoarse, and its volume a whisper.

With faux sympathy, the princess said, "Do you think any human male could be so beautiful? Five minutes in his presence should be enough to tell you he's from an entirely different world. And that's why he's a Vampire Hunter."

Pondering the ghastly implications of the words the princess had uttered with such weight, Elena began to feel dizzy. How could the person who was going to dispose of the Nobility so easily be half vampire himself?

"We're here," the princess exclaimed, the doors before her opening at the sound of her voice.

The trio stepped into a lavishly appointed room. Once they'd taken their seats around a marble table, semitransparent stewards came over without a sound and poured wine into goblets wrought of pure silver.

"I had been thinking about tea," the princess said, "but this is a more grown-up taste. It may be a bit too mature for our young miss, though."

"What, this crap?!" Elena sneered, and she was about to drain the cup when D put his hand across the top of it.

"Let's hear what you have to say. Before anyone drinks anything."

"Are you trying to tell me the battle will be on as soon as we're done drinking? Well, don't worry on that account. I'll gladly indulge you. Are you incapable of taking a simple invitation to tea at face value?"

"Yes."

"How unfortunate that you've had such a poor upbringing," the princess remarked with a wink at Elena, but the biker turned away in disgust. Nonchalantly taking a sip from her cup, the enchanting princess let out a sad sigh and said, "There's something I'd like you to do for me." Her words were directed at D. "It's about my four guardians—although you've only seen three of them so far. I don't suppose you'd be so kind as to dispose of them?"

Silence fell.

Still in the process of bringing the cup to her lips, Elena had her eyes open as wide as they would go. She looked extremely uncomfortable. Born and raised in the village, she was all too familiar with the four knights and their relationship with the princess. If the princess was the moon, then the four knights were the darkness that allowed her radiance to reach the earth. At her bidding, the knights would gallop out like thunder on their chargers, racing off to trample all those who would oppose her.

Ironically enough, it also meant that at times the knights defended the village of Sacri. Elena herself knew of more than a dozen times when various monsters or bands of well-armed brigands had attacked, trying to get at their rich supply of grain. And it was said there'd been countless other attempts in the past. Burn, pillage, and kill—this was the standard under which their villainous attackers gathered, but they'd always been repelled by a hair's breadth and then made the victims of their very own motto by the four knights acting on the princess's orders.

And it was the four knights who boldly thundered out across the plains to challenge the gigantic "earth devourer" that could swallow a whole hill in the course of a night, eventually slaying the beast after a fierce and bloody conflict.

And when the land tsunami that unavoidably crushed everything in its path and churned the debris high into the air was bearing down on the village, it was the knights who arrived like a four-colored wind and used the Nobility's civil engineering equipment and advanced technology to temporarily hide the entire community deep in the earth to keep it safe.

The skillful Hunters who'd come to dispose of the lovely princess residing in this lonely outpost had never managed to breach the doors to her fortress before being cut down amid the whistling blows of her guardians' swords and lances.

The strange thing was, Elena had never actually seen the princess in the flesh before—nor had the mayor or any of the other village elders. When they'd been born, the lady of the manor was already the stuff of legend. The only reason she remained painfully carved into the hearts of the people was because when the knights occasionally called on the village, they often mentioned the princess and delivered her edicts.

Just how old was this woman they called their princess? What were these knights who could walk in the light of the sun?

These questions were always on the tips of the people's tongues, but ultimately sank back into the dark recesses of their brains unanswered. Living as she did in a manor far older than the village, there was no point in asking her age. Most likely, several generations of knights had fought from beneath that immutable armor. After all, it only stood to reason the Noblewoman would need someone of human blood to guard her coffin by day. Needless to say, the Nobility were objects of fear and hatred, and the princess was no exception. At one time, young people and even children had vanished from the village every night, irrespective of sex. They returned with teeth marks on their necks; pale and less than human. Every last one of them had the aroma of roses on their breath, and rose petals filled their pockets. Thus, the lady of the manor became known as "the rose princess."

And yet, incredibly few people had ever offered her any resistance. Aside from the fact she was shielded by her knights, the human populace of this region had a more deeply rooted fear of the Nobility than people in other Frontier sectors. Mothers could only weep as their children were locked up on the edge of town, and husbands drowned their anger in liquor after driving stakes through the hearts of wives who'd bared their fangs. Once in a very great while, a brave rebel would take the road up to the manor, but many of them were never seen again—as if swallowed by the darkness—while even more had been left as brutalized corpses decorating the sides of the road out of town.

It was a few years earlier that the first symptoms of change had manifested. Young people had been born without the innate fear of the Nobility many believed had been fused into their very genetic code. And once grown, they made little secret of their plans to resist the princess and her guardians. Elena was one such person; the dangerous nucleus of her biker group.

"Just what the hell are you up to?" she asked the princess, her voice a mix of tension and trepidation—and expectation.

"They're a hindrance, the lot of them," the lovely princess replied, but her words were directed to D, as always. "The fact of the matter is, I've finally grown tired of these lands. Although I look young, I've actually been here for a fairly long time. And recently, I've yearned to see something of the world at long last. But when I go, I'd like to spread my wings and fly solo. And that's where *they* become a problem."

Elena also looked at D. She couldn't help but wonder what he thought of the staggering information the princess had just disclosed. Relief and excitement filled the biker's heart, but D's expression hadn't changed in the least. No matter what the Nobility had in mind, the Hunter would no doubt remain impassive as he brought all their plans to naught. Beautifully and emotionlessly.

"They are certain to insist on accompanying me," the princess continued. "After all, they live solely to protect me and my stronghold. Doesn't that sound absolutely dismal? I've always been sickened by that cloying kind of love and feelings of loyalty."

"Then why have you put up with it for so long?" D asked.

The princess let a wry smile drift to her lips as she replied, "Oh, there are any number of reasons. Bound by the traditions of my ancestors and so on. They are my retainers, ultimately. It wouldn't do for me to leave them with nothing to do, would it? After all, they haven't a talent for anything but this work."

"But you'd abandon them now that you're bored?"

"Don't make it sound so sordid. Everyone has a right to put their own happiness first, right? I have a feeling that in that respect, humans and Nobles don't differ in the least."

There was no reply.

"That's all I had to say. If you'd be so good as to eliminate them, I'll move on to a different area. And the village will be free—won't it? Everything works out nice and neatly that way. And you can finish up here without even having to destroy me."

"I listened to what you had to say," D said softly.

"Now, hold it right there," the princess said, fairly admonishing the Hunter.

The ghastly aura that'd begun to permeate the area left Elena unable to speak.

"Wait just a moment," the princess continued. "I told you I'd be willing to leave these lands. There's no need for you to try and kill me, is there? Are you some kind of homicidal maniac?"

"I'm a Hunter," D said. Perhaps even that brief response was only out of politeness.

The flash of silver that shot out bisected the lovely princess once, slicing the table in two as well.

"Well done," the princess said, rising completely unscathed.

A stark light mowed through her waist.

In her white dress, she flowed to the center of the room like a fog.

"See, I knew you were pigheaded. If you are intent on fulfilling your contract to slay me, it seems I have no recourse but to change the mind of your employer. But first, watch this."

The princess raised one hand. What then suddenly formed in the air was an image of the village of Sacri as seen from a distance. The silver disc that glowed in the sky was obscured by the fluttering of black wings.

"Bats?!" Elena exclaimed.

As if taking their cue from the biker's cry, the countless winged mammals dove straight for the village.

The view changed.

Elena had her eyes glued to it, for the tiny descending creatures had become roses beyond number. Flowers in four shades billowed ornately down the streets and alleyways. And before the eyes of the awestruck Elena, the image vanished.

"This is not a dream, I tell you. All of that actually happened. Aren't you at all curious what'll become of the village I've blessed with my flowers?"

"What have you done? What the hell were those flowers?!" Elena cried.

"You'll see when you get back there, little girl," the princess replied, her lips remaining parted for silent laughter. "I had intended to kill you here, but now you may return to the village. However, you'll find there are some cases where it's more painful to live than to die. Go ahead and find out for yourself. See exactly what I mean."

As the princess spun around and raced for the door on the far side of the chamber, a stark needle pierced her back. Her laughter never abating, the figure in white was swallowed by fog before she reached the door.

At the same time, the same door that they'd entered by opened to the rear of her two guests. No doubt it was the princess's way of ordering them to leave.

"Let's go back, D," Elena urged the Hunter.

But D walked off toward where the princess had disappeared.

"Where are you going?"

"If you won't go home alone, come with me. Or stay right here, if you like."

Elena's eyes bulged in her sockets, but it only took the blink of an eye for her astonishment to become anger.

Pointing toward the door, she said, "You saw those roses, didn't you? Something really awful is happening back in the village. The only thing that can save someone from being harmed by a Noble is another Noble. And you're half one, right?" Elena exclaimed, but only as the words were coming out of her mouth did she realize what she was saying.

Putting her fist to her mouth, she said, "I'm so sorry."

D had already been swallowed by the fog.

Realizing the gorgeous man and woman were truly creatures from a whole other world, Elena was plunged into a solitude that rent her soul.

II

Elena couldn't even remember how she'd gotten out of the manor. The next thing she knew, the rose garden spread before her like something out of a dream, and a knight sat before her on a black horse. The moonlight informed her that the armor encasing him was the same hue as his mount.

As the girl froze in her tracks, the Black Knight indicated the back of his horse and told her, "Get on."

Elena was at a loss for words.

"There's nothing to fear. The princess's orders were that I deliver you safely back to the village. But only in the event that you came out without the Hunter."

"Why?" she asked. Although she'd tried to put some force behind it, her voice quavered.

"She bade me to let you see the village, come what may. And some very dangerous things come out at night in these parts."

"Sounds like not everything's under her control. Are human beings the only thing she can't set free?"

The Black Knight smiled without saying a word.

Noticing that his was not an unsettling grin, Elena pulled herself together once more. Swallowing her saliva, she said, "I'll go back on my own ride. Out of the way."

"In that case, you'll find it right there," the Black Knight said, tossing his chin to the right and ignoring the rude manner in which she'd declined his offer.

Glistening in the moonlight, her motorcycle looked like it was brand new.

"I gave it a tune-up while you were inside," the knight told her. "That was also on instructions from the princess. But even if you're riding back, I'll escort you."

"Do whatever you like," Elena said absentmindedly as she walked over to her bike. It was like a completely different vehicle. The responsiveness of the accelerator and brake, the feel of the spring suspension, the purr of the engine—they'd all been raised to a new level. Elena restrained her own curiosity about how he'd managed so many improvements in such a short time.

But the question that weighed most heavily on Elena's mind was whether this man or his compatriots in the quartet—one of whom had yet to show himself—had any idea of the change that'd come over their proud liege. The princess was certainly a capricious character, but did she actually think the biker wouldn't tell the knights what she knew?

"What a fine mistress you have," the girl said sarcastically once they'd finished coming down the hill. Suddenly, she stood transfixed by a fierce gaze evident even through the dark of night and held her tongue. In a heartbeat, she'd lost all urge to divulge the secret.

Quickly facing forward again, the Black Knight said in a rusty voice, "Never mention the princess again."

Elena thought he was going to follow up with a threat of some sort, but the knight continued to advance on his steed without saying another word.

"You and your friends will be finished soon," the incorrigible Elena sneered, even though she realized it was a reckless thing to do. "I'm sure he's gonna kill you all. You could all come at him at once and it still wouldn't make any difference."

"You're probably right."

The knight conceded so easily, it threw Elena into a strange mood. Her bike was creeping forward at a speed of about two miles per hour. To be honest, the reason she didn't just take off was because she was scared. Although this knight in black was the most human of the four in his emotions, she was still chilled to the marrow just knowing he was there by her side. And it wasn't horror that chilled her, but rather a physical coldness from the supernatural aura given off by all those in league with the Nobility.

"Then why don't you all take off out of here as fast as you can? And take your mistress with you."

"I believe I just told you I wouldn't allow any further discussion of the princess," the Black Knight said in a tone that froze Elena's blood. "Do you hate us that much?" he asked, his voice carrying a puff of laughter.

"Of course. How many people do you think have been put on the stakes over the years?"

"That's always been done to make an example of those who would harm the princess. It's unavoidable."

Anger caught hold of Elena.

"Unavoidable?!" she snapped. "Try putting yourself in the shoes of those you killed. Of course, the whole lot of you are half dead already, so you probably wouldn't mind, would you?"

The Black Knight seemed to chuckle softly. "Very good. You're exactly right."

As for the next question, even Elena herself didn't know why she asked it. Nevertheless, she said, "Were you guys human once?"

"What do you think?"

"I don't know—that's why I'm asking."

"If you happen to be around when I die, take my helmet off. Then you'll know."

"Okay. I'm looking forward to it."

The biker was just congratulating herself on her cheeky reply when the Black Knight rode past her on one side.

After he'd gone about fifteen feet ahead of her, he asked, "Can you speed up?"

"I only need a half second, and then I'm good to go!"

The two of them were approaching the road that ran straight into the village. To either side, black tree trunks stretched up to the sky. But one of the trees in the stand seemed to be sort of twisted out of shape, and it made Elena blink. Come to think of it, she'd taken this road hundreds of times. There'd never been a tree like that before.

Elena was bracing herself to say something when another tree shot across her field of view. It hadn't fallen. It'd leaned over, and was going right for the Black Knight's head.

The girl saw a band of light. It flowed up from the Black Knight's back to wind around the monstrous tree bearing down on him like an avalanche, and then the bizarre creature fell to the ground, sliced in half where the band of light had touched it.

"Go!" the Black Knight bellowed.

Above his head loomed another tree, and this time it had split open from the tip to reveal stark white fangs as it attacked.

It took half a second for her to hit forty miles per hour. A full second later she hit sixty—and Elena and her bike were both propelled forward by a roar. The very instant she passed the Black Knight, Elena caught the band of light once more out of the corner of her eye, but she sped off without so much as a backward glance. And while she didn't look back, she did wonder about the outcome all the way to the village.

The village gates were still open when they greeted Elena. But it was long past the hour when they should've been shut. Something was wrong here.

Fighting the chill against her skin, Elena rode her bike into the village.

In areas where the Nobility remained, people holed up in their houses as soon as the sun went down. While it was natural that there was no one on the streets, the scent of roses filling the night air made Elena tense. Before she knew it, her left hand was massaging the opposite breast in an attempt to ease her apprehension.

Elena peered into the guardhouse to one side of the gate. There was no sign of anyone. The gatekeeper wouldn't go right home after closing the gates–after all, travelers were known to show up suddenly, and express messengers came from the Capital on occasion. The absence of the gatekeeper was fairly strong evidence something wasn't right.

Elena turned forward again. Someone else's face was right in front of her.

Choking back a scream, Elena said, "Miksin?"

That was the name of the one of her gang members. He wore a dazed expression she'd never seen on him before, and it made him look like a specter.

"What the hell happened? And where's Stahl?"

"Don't . . . know . . . ," the stocky little man mumbled, saliva spilling out with the words as he swung his head from side to side. "Oh, that's right . . . He helped . . . bury everyone. Right now, he's digging . . . a hole . . ."

"A hole? What are you talking about?! Snap out of it!"

Grabbing the man by his powerful shoulders, Elena shook him. The head on top of his bull neck snapped back and forth easily, but Miksin didn't offer any resistance. The girl's left hand slipped off Miksin's shoulder and slid right down his back. Elena knew immediately what the soft sensation traveling from her fingers had to be. She spun Miksin around with all her might.

"What in the world . . . ," she muttered.

On the man's broad back—directly above the seventh thoracic vertebra—a symbol of the world of night was blooming in all its crimson glory. The girl tried to yank it out, but only the petals were left in her hand, while the stem remained rooted in the middle of his back.

"Where is everyone, Miksin? Tell me!" she shouted, but just then the sound of hoof beats reached her ears. "D?!" she said, her assessment all too natural under the circumstances.

"I see you made it back safely," the Black Knight said from outside the gates. His armor had a white luster to it—the work of the moonlight.

"You of all people must know something about what's happened here, right?" Elena asked in a low voice as she pulled her hands away from Miksin. "Tell me. What do we have to do to save everyone? How are we supposed to get these flowers out of them? Tell me, damn you!"

The girl sounded like she was spitting up blood as she beseeched him, but the Black Knight sat there listening like a lump of cold steel.

"My work is done," was all he said as he wheeled his horse around.

"Wait! Wait just a second!" Elena shouted, and at just that moment an idea sparked in her brain, as if by a miracle.

Leaving Miksin behind, the girl dashed out through the gates.

"I'm outside the village now. I'm not safely inside. You haven't fulfilled your duty yet."

"Enough of your childish games," the Black Knight said as he continued to ride away.

"I'm gonna stay out here until you do something. In another minute or so, the beasties will catch my scent and come after me. And if I were to die outside the village, that'd mean you disregarded your princess's commands, wouldn't it?"

Elena had ample confidence in that last comment.

Sure enough, it hit the mark. Certainly this must've been the first time anyone had ever made the Black Knight turn his mount around not once, but twice.

As he rode over to Elena, he remarked, "A crude but effective ploy." He said the words without any modulation, but his delivery alone spoke volumes about Elena's victory. "However, I'm not about to do anything," he added. "What has happened to the village is in accordance with the will of the princess."

"Which would you choose?" Elena asked, desperately trying to retain the upper hand. "To be punished for killing me, or to be scolded for preventing some evil work of the princess that you had no part in? If I were you, I'd see to it that I did my job."

"I'm not going to move from this spot," said the Black Knight. "But I shall be here all night to cut down anything that tries to attack you. Stay right there, if you wish."

Elena realized he'd turned the situation around. With despair and rage blasting through every inch of her, the biker stomped her feet and shouted, "If you walk around in the daylight, you can't be a Noble! What are you, a synthetic human? Well, no matter what you are, if you're even remotely human, there's no way you could just leave the village to its fate. If you believe in following orders, you must be capable of respecting others. In that case, you've also gotta be able to understand their suffering!"

Elena's reasoning was a bit forced, but it was all she could think of at the moment. To be honest, she didn't believe it would have any effect at all.

As expected, the Black Knight didn't budge an inch. He had become a statue, sitting there on his horse, devoid not only of emotion but of life itself.

"You heartless monster! Fine. I won't ask any more of you. Take off already." The girl turned and was about to walk back in through the gates.

"Wait," a voice called out behind her.

Another reversal—but Elena couldn't focus on her own joy at this turn of events as she'd noticed a number of figures heading toward her from the village.

III

It wasn't Miksin, but she was only sure of that after she noticed the five or six villagers who had also drawn the Black Knight's attention.

"Look over there . . . That's Elena, isn't it?" an old woman thin as a withered tree branch said with obvious joy.

"That's right. It's Elena," said another. "You're unharmed, I see."

"We can share this with you. Join us."

Beslik, dressed in his butcher's apron, and the old man who ran the general store clawed at the air like they were swimming as they approached her.

Elena swore she could hear all the blood draining from her body like a tide. She was looking at *things* that wore faces all too familiar to her.

She got them, the girl thought with horror. *But something's wrong. It's so . . . indiscriminate. Up until now, she's only preyed on young people.*

"Stand back," someone bellowed, but Elena found it difficult to believe it was the Black Knight. Weren't the creatures before her eyes the very same thing as the princess? Elena backed away three steps, while the Black Knight rode forward three.

Instinctively curious about the man's weapon, Elena looked at his back and saw an iron sheath roughly two feet long. Or rather, there were two scabbards for two broadswords there, and it looked like one was laid on top of the other. Rough in size and shape, the weapons didn't seem at all suitable for this giant.

It came as little surprise that the trio of villagers were taken aback when they came out through the gates, but they must've viewed the knight as an ally, as they quickly spread their arms and started walking toward Elena.

A horizontal flash of light mowed through the napes of their necks.

Elena was reminded of champagne corks shooting off from the internal pressure. But instead of fermented fruit juice and gas, the three necks were sending geysers of blackish blood into the air. Beyond brutal, beyond gruesome, the scene could've even been termed striking by some, but it left Elena so totally unnerved that even when she heard the blades being sheathed, she didn't turn toward the swordsman.

Undoubtedly the Black Knight had utilized the weapons from his back. But how? He'd sat on his horse without lifting a finger, and even if he'd extended his arm, his weapon never would've reached the closest villager, let alone all three of them.

Apparently the stroke had been so masterful the trio didn't even realize they'd been cut, and they took two or three more sure-footed steps before collapsing limply.

The sight of the falling bodies finally brought Elena back to her senses.

"What the hell are you doing?!" the biker shouted, glaring at the Black Knight.

"They were going after you," he replied. There was laughter in his voice, but the flustered Elena didn't notice it.

"You didn't have to kill them. I—I mean, there's gotta be some way to save them."

"Once they're like that, there's but one way to 'save them,' as you put it."

Elena's chest grew tight at the Black Knight's reply. It was exactly as he said. The only "salvation" for a human who'd been made a servant of the Nobility was the kind the Black Knight had dispensed.

"But why? They were your mistress's . . ."

"Never."

"What?" Elena said, her eyes going wide.

"The princess would never do such a thing. The very thought of her elevating you humans to the same state as herself, even as her servants—there must be some mistake."

"Oh, it's no mistake, mark my—"

The rest of Elena's words were crushed by the black figure's advance. Feeling the same pressure as if a mountain was moving by, Elena stepped to one side.

"I must rectify this error," the Black Knight said before he passed through the gates.

"Wait!" Elena cried, bounding out in front of his horse.

"Out of my way. You're in the village now. It's no longer my responsibility whether you live or die."

"Are you planning on killing everyone here? I can't let you do that."

"And you intend to stop me?" the Black Knight asked, his voice dropping lower.

"I sure do," Elena replied from a spot ten feet away.

The wind snarled. The skill the girl displayed in pulling her chain free and swinging it around as she leapt out of the way was truly impressive, but how much good her weapon would do against the heavily armored Black Knight was the real question. And her motorcycle wasn't nearby.

There was a sharp rap as sparks flew from the Black Knight's helm. The weight on the chain had scored a direct hit, and more hits came in rapid succession. This rustic lass had taken that single length of chain and made it seem more like a dozen weapons, simply with the skilled manipulations of one hand. And when the knight's upper body swayed, Elena brought her left hand into play, too. As the second chain swept the front legs out from under it, the horse toppled forward.

The knight's massive form rose. The laws of physics should've launched his body forward, or perhaps it would've been even more appropriate for him to touch down feet-first, as light as a feather, behind Elena. But the skill of the woman warrior had seen to it that chains were wound about both his wrists. Moreover, when Elena raised her hands, the weights at the other end of the chains angled up into the air, wrapping around the heavy branches of the colossal trees that towered to either side of the knight and robbing him of his freedom.

"Just stay there and behave yourself," Elena said as she dashed toward her bike.

From behind her, a low voice called out, "What will you do now?"

Ignoring the query, she hopped onto her bike and started the engine. The only thing that kept her level-headed was the fact that the Black Knight's voice hinted at mocking laughter when he'd called out to her. Although she wasn't sure whether the laser generator set inside her headlight would prove effective or not, Elena didn't have any other options.

"Watch this, missy!" the Black Knight exclaimed.

Elena saw him tug on his fully extended arms. The branches snapped, and the crimson beam split the darkness as it blazed at the Black Knight. Tree branches rained down from either side to block the laser.

A wind and a rumbling of the earth sent Elena and her bike flying, but it wasn't from branches. Rather, she was sent into the air by the thud from the trunks of the gargantuan trees that'd fallen over. The Black Knight had torn them up, roots and all, with consummate ease. The trees rested against the rows of houses to either side, their trunks forming double fences while a composed voice called from behind them, "Well then, here I go. Off to correct all the mistakes. You should be thankful these trees have saved your life."

"Wait!" Elena shouted as she was about to start her bike, but then she received a shock.

The two tree trunks seemed to have been purposely placed in an arrangement calculated to keep her bike from ever getting between them.

"Damn it all!" Elena snarled, slamming her fist into the palm of her other hand. But she quickly decided on her course of action.

Freeing the chain from a branch of the nearer tree, she then wrapped it firmly around the trunk, pulled it taut, and looped it around an iron stake driven deep into the ground. The stake was one she'd had in the storage compartment on her bike.

Having backed up as far as the gates, Elena hunkered down over the handlebars wearing an expression that brimmed with impatience and self-confidence. The exhaust pipes spat flames. Steered with miraculous skill, the bike barreled up the thin line she'd strung from the tree to the ground, flying high into the air to effortlessly clear the two trunks and land on the darkened street beyond.

Taking a hard bounce as they came back to earth, Elena and her bike knifed through the wind now that the last obstacle had been cleared, and a few seconds later they sped into the square.

An unexpected sight greeted the warrior woman. A well was situated at the center of the square, and by it stood the Black Knight with a tiny, frail figure.

"Mama Kipsch!" Elena cried, her voice carrying an added weight. While she realized the village was in great peril, the name she'd said was the only reason even a hint of reassurance lingered in her heart.

"Welcome back," the silver-maned crone replied without ever looking at Elena. An earthen pot was cradled under her left arm. Her right hand was sunk into its wide mouth up to the elbow.

Turning her eyes in the same direction both of the others faced, Elena had her breath taken away. In the moonlight, it looked like the villagers lay on the ground, piled one on top of the other. None of them were moving at all. Worse yet, the sight of a number of others crawling into the open holes that riddled the ground gave Elena goose bumps. Was this what Miksin had been talking about?

Looking up at the Black Knight, Mama Kipsch said, "So, how about it?"

"Very well. As promised, I shall wait three days. And during that time—you know what you're to do, don't you?"

"Not a problem. I'll keep my end of the deal, too."

Elena suddenly felt like her own deadly battle with the knight was something that'd happened a whole world away.

Silently climbing onto his jet black mount, the Black Knight then said, "Well, I'm off—but the humans truly don't deserve such a great witch doctor." With those words, he wheeled his horse around.

As the knight and his mount passed right by the end of her nose, Elena could only stand and watch like a demented soul.

The horse halted. Up on its back, the Black Knight merely turned his head a bit to gaze at Elena. White moonlight gleamed off his helm and pauldrons, making him look like a sculpture from another dimension.

"We shall meet again—soldier!" he told her.

And then his horse's hooves tore into the dirt as he galloped off down the street.

When a hand came to rest on Elena's shoulder, the biker returned to her senses. Mama Kipsch's mournful countenance greeted her. Before Elena could say a word, the elderly witch doctor who'd just sent a killer packing said, "You threw down with him, did you?"

"Yeah."

"Must've been a good fight."

"How do you know that?" asked the girl.

"You heard what he said, 'soldier.' It would seem he's taken a shine to you."

"Spare me, Mama Kipsch. Anyway, what the hell was all this . . . ," Elena began to say, but when she'd surveyed the whole square, she then let out a little whoop of joy. People had appeared from some of the neighboring houses.

"There are some folks the flowers didn't get, though that's less than a tenth of the populace, I warrant."

"And all the rest have joined the Nobility?"

Mama Kipsch nodded, and for a moment Elena's head began to swim. The only thing that kept her from fainting was the old woman's next remark.

"But that's not to say they've gone over *completely*. After all, they haven't been bitten. We should be able to do something for them."

At the crone's doleful expression, Elena was forced to swallow the next thing she wanted to say.

In just three days?

D was in a fog.

An hour had already elapsed since he'd first started after the princess. Elena hadn't come with him, but he didn't appear at all concerned by that.

D didn't actually know where he was, as surprising as that might seem. Though the gorgeous Hunter was part vampire, his sense of direction had become horribly confused. But what was truly scary about the young man was how he didn't seem to rely on it at all. The fact was, he wasn't wading through a cloud of complete darkness. The fog carried a fragrance—that of a rose. Without a doubt, it had to belong to the lovely princess. The scents of other roses swirled through the fog as well. And yet, there was no uncertainty in D's gait.

"You happen to know where we are?" the Hunter's left hand asked. It sounded anxious.

But what could leave the hand so frightened?

D didn't reply, and perhaps that added to the left hand's anxiety, because it continued, "Now I'm sure you don't have a clue, but—"

"We're six hundred feet underground," said D.

"Sheesh!" the hand spat in reply. "You mean to tell me you don't know where we're going, but you still know how far down we are? You're an odd one. Well, what have we here?"

D had already noticed, too—the fog was clearing. The white mass was drifting away, becoming a thin band that unraveled, coiled, and vanished like the threads of a spider's web. And from beyond the fog appeared a bottomless darkness.

"It stinks like hell down here," the left hand stated.

Having lost the scent of roses, the air and darkness were now choked with the nauseating stench of corruption.

"It's not a room—it's more like a root cellar, I'd say. As far as the dimensions go, it stretches about six miles across and goes about a hundred fifty feet high. Wild animals probably live here. Still, it's awfully quiet. I don't sense a single—"

Before the hand could say, "thing," the sound of creaking gears traveled down through the darkness that loomed over them like the heavens.

As D looked up, his eyes must've caught something, because just as his cool black pupils came to rest on a certain spot on the floor, there was a juicy *plop!*

Something had dropped from the ceiling. And the room above the ceiling was apparently shrouded in darkness.

D started off through the pitch blackness without any sign of agitation. But not toward where the thing had fallen. He was following the scent of flowers that lingered despite the putrid stench. The lovely princess was to be destroyed— nothing else interested D. But was it mere coincidence that the thin thread of fragrance led him right to where the massive sack lay on the floor?

"There's raw meat inside," the left hand said. "A whole ton, roughly."

A rank odor spilled from the mouth of the bag.

"I'm sure you already know, but I smell something else, too. And it's—," the voice began to say, the words flowing off to the right.

As D was in motion, two bits of darkness came from either side of him and overlapped before his nose. From the spot where they'd landed, shrill cries arose. Although it was unclear if this was the sound of a man or a beast, D's eyes confirmed the presence of tiny creatures armed with equally diminutive blades about ten feet from him on either side. Their little fishhook claws and tiny bat-like wings were more cute than menacing, but the creatures' ability was made manifest by strands of black hair that continued to fall from D's brow.

Crimson points of light began to glow. They were the eyes of homunculi, spiteful blood-light spilling from faces covered with lumps.

Thin glimmers flew at D from all sides. Short spears aimed at him, though they were so tiny as to hardly even qualify as spears. The hem of the Hunter's coat whirled out to fend off the missiles, but a second later the garment was rent in an "x" shape. A tiny assassin who'd flown at him with the fusillade of spears had deftly laid into it with his blade.

Preparing to launch a new assault, the second wave of creatures was coiled to pounce when their crimson eyes bulged in their sockets. Just as the two homunculi from the vanguard had landed, they'd split in half lengthwise. Screeching cries of astonishment intertwined, fading off into the distance like ripples on a pond. But then they stopped dead.

With his naked blade in one hand, D slowly turned his whole body to face the way he'd come. Something enveloped his entire frame, and his left hand gasped in surprise.

An eerie miasma likely to leave all who felt it dead or disabled was billowing from the depths of the darkness. There was an intensity to it that was completely unlike that of the three knights he'd met in the world above—and yet there was also a strange similarity. This was the fourth—the last of what people called the "Four Knights of the Diane Rose."

The source of the eerie emanations had moved. It was headed of the depths of the vast darkness. Several seconds later, the presence he'd detected became the sounds of hooves. Perhaps it was the weird atmosphere of the place that made the echoes of kicked-up soil warp into torpid, drawn-out sounds.

D didn't move. With his blade in his right hand, he waited somberly for his foe.

The sound stopped. Fifteen feet lay between it and D.

"What have we here?" a strangely lisping voice called down from high on a mount. "I came looking for my meal and *opponents*. But the princess has played a cruel trick on me . . . Who knew there were still men of such beauty in the world?"

D was now gazing at the knight in white armor who sat before him on a white steed. Or perhaps it would've been better to say the Hunter's eyes were facing straight ahead, and it just happened that the horse and rider filled his field of vision. Though even his left hand was enveloped in the eerie aura, the figure of beauty showed not a glimmer of tension.

"I'm so pleased," said the knight. The longsword on his left hip shook ever so slightly. "It's been a long time . . . since my heart raced so. There's a fire in my chest . . . I hear a beating that was supposedly silenced more than five centuries ago . . . Oh, yes . . . Yes . . ."

His sword sang out once more. The White Knight's upper body trembled with delight. The words spilled from his lips as if he couldn't push them out fast enough.

"Do you want to cut him down, 'Slayer'? Do you want to slice into this gorgeous man? I know . . . But just wait . . . We'll save that pleasure for later . . . First, we must do our daily cleaning . . ."

The White Knight extended his left arm and began to beckon to the homunculi with his hand. Languidly. Gently. Like a pale resident of the afterworld beckoning the living.

"Come," he said. "Come . . . foes that the princess has granted me . . . Oh, it seems today . . . we have a lively bunch . . ."

A streak of light pierced the white body, and with the hurled spear, the tiny murderers pounced on him from all sides. They were consumed, deadly weapons and all, by a wave of white. The movement of the wave resembled the hand that'd called them forward. When it opened once more, the short spears had all been knocked to the ground and the four homunculi had been sliced in half at the waist horizontally, as if in answer to D's vertical cuts earlier.

"Come," he said as he beckoned to his next opponents—the only ones who remained.

Three tiny figures zipped at the figure on horseback. Although they were moving at different speeds and flying at varied altitudes, a flash of white light mowed through their torsos, leveling all three of them at once.

"My cape . . . wasn't cut . . . ," the White Knight muttered.

Only after he'd finished did the six pieces of sundered flesh fall to the ground. And more horrible than the sight of them was the sound they made as they struck the earth.

"Not good . . . Not good at all . . . I went through them much faster . . . than I would've liked," the White Knight said, the words coming out in a pant. His right hand returned the longsword to his hip as he continued, "And it's all your fault. You're that striking . . . That powerful . . . Oh, you wicked man . . . Now I must introduce you to 'Slayer.'"

A tiny metallic rasping rose from the knight's hip. The sound was so disturbing that if there'd been anyone else to hear it, they would've curled up in a ball and covered their ears. The sword and scabbard were rubbing against each other. All by itself, the blade was sliding out of its sheath, then back, only to repeat the whole process again and again—as if it hadn't done enough cutting, or spilled enough blood. As if it was too soon for it to settle back into its scabbard. After all, D was still there, wasn't he?

So, this blade was "Slayer."

Into the Forest of Death

CHAPTER 4

I

The warriors stood facing each other in the darkness for a few seconds—the rasping of Slayer in its sheath the only sound to be heard—while a murderous intent no one save these two could sense continued to build. When they crossed naked steel, who would prove the better man? D's coat had been cut by the attacks of the vicious, nimble little homunculi, while the White Knight's cape had remained unscathed. What's more, it seemed Slayer itself was imbued with some sort of magic.

The silence was broken by the White Knight as he said, "Time to draw you, Slayer."

The blade danced out. The motion was so smooth, it looked as if the sword had leapt into the knight's hand rather than waiting to be drawn.

D, on the other hand, wasn't poised for action—he had neither relaxed nor tensed his body, and his arms hung by his sides.

"You're good . . . ," said the White Knight. "Simply by standing there, you're nearly enough to make my blood freeze. I doubt I shall ever again face such an opponent in a battle of life or death."

The knight suddenly wheeled his horse around. Without a backward glance he rode on, the hoofbeats growing fainter and fainter.

Though his foe's actions were perplexing, D didn't move from where he stood.

What was he waiting for?

The dwindling hoofbeats began to ring louder and stronger. The rider was coming back. And as the strides of the approaching mount resounded, they echoed a faint yet unshakable determination to kill.

He kept coming. One hundred fifty feet . . . One twenty-five . . . One hundred . . .

D was motionless.

The rider's blade would come crashing down like a tidal wave. But what would happen when it was met by another sword whipping up from the ground like a gust of snow and ice?

Thirty feet . . . Fifteen . . . Ten . . .

The gorgeous form was eclipsed by a massive figure and the wild pounding of hooves. And then—there was the most gorgeous chime in the world, and a flash of white flew off like a shooting star.

Who would've thought that D's blade would snap off at the hilt?

Sparks shooting from his horse's hooves as it came to a sudden stop, the White Knight turned and laughed.

"No blade can stand up to Slayer," he said. "Now you're finished."

And what did D do? He remained in the same spot while the enchanted blade once again groaned through the air, this time aimed at the Hunter's skull.

A bloody spray shot out.

"Oh!" the knight cried in surprise when he felt his sword do something other than sink into flesh.

Slayer's blade was pinned between the palms of the hands D had clapped together over his head. However, a dark liquid was also gushing from those same hands. The Hunter's own fresh blood rained down on his forehead, streaming down the side of his nose.

Slayer sank a bit deeper.

"Die, damn you! Die! All who do battle with the Slayer die," the White Knight bellowed, his eyes tinged red with insanity.

Was this knight's strength actually a match for D's? Or was it his sword's enchantment that gave him the edge? The blade was slowly sliding down between the palms of D's hands, releasing a shower of blood on the Hunter in the process.

Screeching like a crazed raptor, the White Knight let his cry become the force behind his blade as he brought it down. His bloodshot eyes reflected a hue that was far deeper. Yes, D's eyes. The blood that'd coursed down off the Hunter's forehead ran in a crimson line to his lips.

D pivoted.

"Oof!" the knight exclaimed, the cry stretching from the back of the mount he'd been sitting on to the spot fifteen feet away where he thudded to earth again.

As D prepared to stalk over to the fallen knight, a gigantic white form leapt in front of him—the White Knight's steed. It stood stock still, blocking the way.

"Outstanding!" the knight exclaimed with apparent pleasure from where he lay, and his horse dashed over to him at full speed. Gory blade dangling limply from one hand, the White Knight grabbed the reins that hung by him and finally managed to pull himself up. Giving a rough shake to his head, he said, "You're a powerful brute. I believe I may have broken some bones . . . It can't be . . . that you descend from the same sort of blood as our princess . . . You're the Vampire Hunter I heard about . . . aren't you?"

"How right you are!" a voice cried from the darkness. Needless to say, it was that of the princess. She sounded like a little flirt, but her presence had gone undetected by the White Knight, and even D himself hadn't noticed her.

"Oh, my . . . Princess . . . ," the knight stammered. As demented as he seemed to be, his mistress apparently merited special treatment. Putting Slayer back on his hip, he went down on one knee, his head already bowed. Evincing not a trace of madness or mockery, the act was one of pure loyalty.

With a dance-like movement the pale and lovely princess appeared from a spot about fifteen feet to the left of the Hunter.

"Well, I trust you had an interesting experience, did you not, my White Knight?" said the princess. If ever a face glowed, hers did now.

"Yes, milady," the knight replied succinctly, sounding like a completely new man.

"There are men of such power out in the world. I wonder if even your Slayer could best him."

The white helm rose.

"Begging your pardon, but I believe you'll find—"

The princess hastily waved her hands, saying, "You needn't say a thing. I was mistaken, and please forget I mentioned it. This will be decided at some other time. D, that goes for you, too. Now that you've lost your sword, you couldn't possibly go on," she said, but as her eyes studied D's profile, the fear in them was evident.

D's eyes were ablaze with blood. Still empty-handed, he advanced.

"Don't stalk over to me with that frightful expression. Off with you!" the princess said as she backed away. "Why don't you go back to the village instead? The flowers I scattered there should be causing quite a furor."

A whistle pierced the air.

"Princess!" the White Knight exclaimed, deftly drawing his blade and cutting down the rough wooden needle.

However, the reason the princess moaned as she pressed down on the left side of her chest was because another needle had eluded her knight and penetrated not her breast, but the back of her hand.

"Isn't that something," she said with a grin, no doubt highly appreciative of the way the Hunter had managed to get one of his missiles past Slayer, although the lovely princess's skill in narrowly stopping the needle he'd just thrown with her bare hands had probably impressed D in return.

Still, a second later the hem of the gorgeous Hunter's coat billowed out as he dashed at the lovely vampire princess.

The White Knight was ready to meet him.

It was just then that the earth rumbled. Six hundred feet underground, the floor of this subterranean chamber was braced by an unspeakable mass of earth, yet it thrashed like a giant serpent.

D's body flew into the air and was swallowed by the darkness before it ever touched the floor.

Light had returned. D was surrounded by a sea of stars.

"Looks like we're okay," said the Hunter's left hand. It didn't sound at all apprehensive. If anything, its tone could've been described as matter-of-fact.

Giving no reply, D surveyed his surroundings. The darkness was almost kin to the young man.

He was on top of a huge rounded stone. A long line of similar stones continued downward, their faces glimmering in a manner reminiscent of the crescent moon. The lights that flickered far off in the distance must've been those of some community.

"We're on top of a mountain," his left hand said incredulously. "Judging by the strength of the winds and the direction they're blowing, we've gotta be a good two miles up. Looks like our little friend can teleport stuff. Well, she sure caught us napping!"

D was looking up at the stars, but he quickly lowered his eyes again and began making his way down the rocks without a sound. The way he leapt from one rock to the next, he seemed like a master of dance.

Based on the positions of the stars, he must've been at the northern extreme of the princess's domain. It would probably take a whole day and night of hard riding to get back to Sacri.

"That's an interesting tidbit," the old woman said as she tossed a whole bundle of herbs into the dirty brown liquid boiling in her cauldron.

They were in the dispensary she ran out of a back room in her house. Not one of the village mayors had ever seen the inside of it, and as Elena stood there by the crone's side telling her all about what had transpired at the castle, she was actually the first visitor the room had seen in fifty years. The noon daylight speared the sooty lace curtains.

"To think that the princess would ask the Hunter to get rid of her four knights. Well, anyone as handsome as him could probably do it, too."

As the conversation seemed like it was about to take a strange turn, Elena tried to get it back on track, saying, "I thought you'd be more surprised, Mama Kipsch. I mean, the princess asked him to *kill her knights*, of all things! What the hell could she be plotting?"

"She's not plotting anything," the aged witch doctor said purposefully as she took three tablespoons of red powder from a glass jar and added them to her pot. "She's probably telling the truth."

"You mean she seriously wants them dead? Why?!"

"For the very reason you said. I suppose she wants to be free now."

"The Nobility abandoning one of their castles?" Elena said. Shrugging her shoulders, she continued, "I've never heard of such a thing. They're connected to their fortresses, like light to shadow. One can't exist without the other. Isn't that why we've been put through hell?"

"There is no hell," Mama Kipsch muttered, her tone once again heavy with meaning. "We humans grow some odd ducks. Like you, or my grandson. It's not so strange to suppose it's the same for the Nobility. After all, they look pretty much the same as we do."

"Then that bitch might really mean it . . . ," Elena muttered. Mama Kipsch was the village's great repository of wisdom, and her words made the girl finally appreciate the grave import of what the princess had said.

"But listen—you're not to mention that to anyone else," the witch doctor said, her forcefulness bringing Elena back to her senses.

"Why's that?"

"Because in this village, there are those who wouldn't be too happy with the news."

A horrible expression briefly passed across Elena's face.

"I suppose you've got a point there."

"But enough about that. Help me think of some way to deal with the crisis at hand. I simply don't have enough blue yaki moss to finish making this medicine," Mama Kipsch said as she folded her arms.

"Blue moss . . . Do you mean the stuff I think you do? From the Shamballa Forest?"

"Oh, forget I mentioned it," the old woman told her. "I'm sure I'll find something else I can use instead."

A thought seemed to occur to Elena, and she said, "There's nothing else to use and you know it. You've always been a lousy liar, you know. Okay, I'll go get it."

"Don't. It's high noon already. Even on your bike it'd be two hours to the forest and another hour to find the moss—You'd be lucky to make it back by five o'clock Night. And the forest is far too dangerous."

"Hell, I'm not going alone. That'd be nuts. I'll bring my boyfriends with me. Luckily, they were off drinking at a warehouse on the edge of town, so some of them didn't get the vampire rose baptism."

"You'll be throwing your lives away," Mama Kipsch told the girl.

"We'll never know if we don't try. Your own grandson lost his life doing what he believed in. And not even for his girlfriend, but for an unrequited love. We all respect the hell out of that."

Turning her eyes to the floor, the old woman then placed a hand on Elena's shoulder and thanked her. "Okay, you'll get some for me then?" she asked.

"Of course. I wanna do whatever I can to make things miserable for those bastards." And with those words, Elena ground her back teeth together as if testing the firmness of her own resolve.

II

Going outside, Elena headed toward the square—it was less than a three-minute walk from Mama Kipsch's house. A hastily improvised tent had been stretched over the spot where so many of the village's

96 | HIDEYUKI KIKUCHI

inhabitants had buried themselves. Needless to say, it was there to ward off the rays of the sun. Though there was a facility for people who'd been turned into Nobility situated on the southern edge of the village, it couldn't begin to accommodate them all. The tent had taken the villagers who remained unaffected a good five hours to put up after sunrise, and it still hadn't been large enough—a third of the covering had been improvised from blankets and fabric.

As she got closer to the tent, odd cries began to beat against her eardrums. Scowling alone wasn't going to accomplish anything, and she didn't want to plug her ears. She had to listen to keep feeding the rage she felt toward the bastards responsible for all those moans.

As one of the villagers standing at the entrance to the tent noticed Elena, his expression grew stern. He adjusted his grip on the spear in his right hand. It was a farmer by the name of Gary.

"I'm not a Noble, you know," Elena said, showing him a smile anyway.

"Why is this happening to us?" Gary asked, his expression unchanged.

"I don't know."

"That young feller comes along and all this shit happens on the same day. Someone saw the two of you taking the road up toward the castle."

"Well, we turned around before we got there," the girl replied. "Since we don't get many lookers like him in town, I thought I'd take him on a little date."

"Bah, you lousy whore," the man spat as he turned away in disgust. No one in the community really appreciated the wild behavior of Elena's group.

"Pardon me," Elena said without letting the expression change on her face, but once she'd slipped in through the flap, she unleashed a vicious kick with her right foot.

As always, her instincts were spot-on. Most likely, not even the rough-and-tumble farmer had ever taken a kick to the genitals through a layer of canvas before. Groans of pain could be heard coming from the ground outside.

"Learn how to talk to a lady, you damn limp dick," said Elena. And though that kick should've lifted her spirits, her voice was heavy.

The moaning in the tent had grown deafening. It took quite an effort on Elena's part just to keep from shutting her eyes.

Half-buried in the earth or caked with dirt, the villagers were writhing on the ground. On their backs, necks, and foreheads, roses of four different colors opened unexpectedly. Even if the villagers who hadn't been afflicted pulled them out, more roses would rise from the sundered flesh to flower in beautiful displays of red, blue, black, and white. Apparently, this abnormal method of infection hadn't made them true servants of the Nobility, as they didn't sleep through the day but rather writhed in agony when the rays of the sun penetrated the thick canvas tarp sheltering them. That was why they were being protected instead of having stakes driven through their hearts, Elena told herself. If these people had received the kiss of the Nobility, they'd have long since been dispatched. It was the law of the Frontier.

"E . . . le . . . na . . . ," a voice sobbed down by her feet.

Saying nothing, Elena just kept looking straight ahead.

"Help . . . It's me . . . Decoy . . ."

"And me . . . Seren . . ."

"It's so hot . . . The pain . . . My body . . . is . . . burning . . ."

Something caught hold of her ankle. A cold hand. Elena didn't move.

"Just wait a little longer. I'm sure we'll get you back to normal." But as the girl spoke, her body trembled. From the ankle in her friend's grip, an evil chill that beggared description was needling into her. Her flesh was starting to crawl. And that voice—

"E . . . le . . . na . . ."

"You damn freak!" she snarled, the words coming out in a tone even she couldn't have imagined. Her right hand slid down to her hip and took a length of weighted chain. She hauled back with it, and then whipped it down hard, all intentionally. A sickening sound was heard, and unpleasantly warm spray flew in her face. But she just kept bringing the weighted end down. Time and again she swung it. And between the blows, the voice continued to call her name faintly, almost as if intoning a curse.

Perhaps that was what the weight on the end of the chain was meant to bring to an end.

Behind her, a different voice cried out, "Elena—What are you doing?!"

A thick arm roughly encircled her torso, dragging her backward.

"Let go of me, you freak! I'll kill you!" she shouted, the last expression echoing out in the sunlight.

"Simmer down, you idiot."

A slap resounded against her cheek.

Now free of whatever had possessed her, Elena stood to one side of the square. Out in front of the tent, Gary was still curled up on the ground, and it was one of the bikers that came out from behind the girl to face her. A single strip of hair that resembled an eclair stretched down the center of his otherwise bald head. It was Stahl, the gang's second-in-command.

Rubbing her cheek, Elena said softly, "That hurt, you know. Care to be a little gentler next time?"

"Sorry about that," Stahl replied, baring his pearly teeth in a smile. His eyes told her, *That's more like it.*

"How many of us are left?" Elena asked him.

"Seven came down with this thing. All that leaves is me, Tan, and Nichou."

"Counting me, that makes four. That'll be enough."

"Enough for what?"

"To go into the Shamballa Forest and find some blue moss," Elena said as she stared off in the exact opposite direction from the Noble's manor.

Her words made Stahl's eyes bulge.

"You mean now? It'll be night by the time we finish!"

"That's a risk I'm willing to take."

"Going out there near dark is just plain suicide," said Stahl. "We'd be throwing our lives away."

"I wish to hell I knew why that's all anyone ever has to say. If your life's that dear to you when push comes to shove, maybe you're not cut out for playing the tough guy even in a little hick village like this. Run on home and hide under your blankets."

"I'm just saying . . ."

"My ears are gonna bleed if I hear any more excuses," the girl told him. "Fine. I'll go by myself."

"And if you get the moss, what happens then?"

"Then everyone goes back to normal—probably. That all depends on Mama Kipsch."

Stahl was at a loss for words.

Turning her back on her still silent compatriot, Elena walked off toward the houses. The only thing on her mind was where she'd be able to find the weapons she'd need. That, and one thing more—the figure of a young man in black whose garments whirled out in the moonlight danced across Elena's eyelids, but she pushed the image to the back of her brain with willpower . . . and perhaps a little sadness.

Racing along at just under a hundred miles per hour for exactly two hours, she could finally see a fog-like blob of black beyond the red clay plains. Just as she was going for the accelerator to increase her speed, she heard the tinny whine of an engine coming up behind her. She rode on regardless, but a few seconds later three more bikes pulled up alongside her so their vehicles advanced in a perfect line.

"Welcome back, wimp," she said, still facing forward.

To her right, Stahl rubbed his own head and said, "Aw, don't say that. I'm here, ain't I?"

"Maybe I should give you a medal or something."

"Cut 'im some slack already, Elena," moon-faced Nichou said from the bike to her left, giving her a wink. Like his face, the man's body was plump and round. "Why didn't you come get us sooner? Me and Tan chewed his ass pretty good, you know."

"Stahl was just worried about all of us," said Tan from the other side of Nichou as a smile rose to his lips. He and Nichou were thick as thieves, but physically they were complete opposites—he was a mass of lean muscle.

"Well, I suppose you didn't want or need me worrying about any of you. Anyway, I don't think even we're low enough that we'd let our leader go off all alone to fetch that stuff," Stahl said, bashfully pawing at his one remaining strip of hair.

Without so much as cracking a grin, Elena said to him, "Just as long as we're clear on that. This might be the only chance we ever get to do something for somebody else. Your lives are in my keeping now."

The only reply she got from her compatriots was the roar of their bikes.

Ten minutes later, the four of them reached the entrance to a forest where massive black boles reached out with branches and leaves the hue of darkness. Finding the thin thread of a footpath that led into the thickly packed forest was simple enough.

"We've got no choice but to leave the bikes here," Elena said as she got out of the saddle.

"Do you even know where this blue moss stuff grows?" Stahl asked as he put a gun that looked more like a cannon and an ammo belt across his back.

Tan unloaded a thick, three-foot-high cylinder with a nozzle from his vehicle, and Nichou walked along lightly while busily rotating both wrists. Around them spun long, thin gleams of light.

"Let's roll!"

At Elena's command, the gleams resolved into three throwing knives in each of Nichou's hands.

There were cracks in the forest canopy that hung over the group like a black cloud, and through them trickled long, thin shafts of light. Although the patterns of sunlight were the product of nature, they possessed such a strangely geometrical order that it was said many traveling artists came to admire them.

As Elena recalled, the blue moss grew on a rock pile in the western part of the forest. Cautiously venturing in further, the group found their entire field of view filled by the great variety of plants that called the forest home.

"Hot damn! Would you look at all that yogari weed, slim green, and stretching bamboo! If we could pick that alone and sell it in the Capital, we'd be living high on the hog for a good six months. A goddamn shame is what it is. You sure we can't stop and pick some?" Tan muttered.

"Every second counts," Elena told him. "Pretty soon, this well-behaved forest is gonna show its ugly side."

But even as she reprimanded her compatriot, Elena couldn't help but share his feelings of what a waste it was to leave such treasures behind.

The vibrantly colored plants Tan had named—and many more—grew in profusion between the trees or among their roots, and all of them were eagerly sought by merchants from the Capital for their medical applications. Even though the nearby village didn't have an appreciable amount of land under cultivation, it was quite wealthy thanks to the bounty of the forest. What's more, due to the special properties of the ozone given off by the trees in the forest and the unique composition of its soil, there were always enough plants regardless of how many were harvested. The path the group was following had actually been worn by people out collecting the various specimens.

"Notice anything, Stahl?" Elena asked nonchalantly after they'd been walking for about three minutes.

"Yep," he replied without as much as a nod of his nearly bald head. "We've had a tail on us for a while. My gut's telling me it could be real trouble."

"No argument there. You suppose it's 'the forest dweller?'"

"Damned if I know. But it's not closing or losing any ground—gotta be pretty smart by the look of things."

Although Tan and Nichou must've been able to hear every word the other two said, they didn't seem at all concerned. After all, these young men had not only grown up on the Frontier, but they'd led a rough-and-tumble life in their gang. It took a lot to unnerve them.

"Should we say hello?"

"Sure," Elena replied, and as she spoke, she snapped her fingers twice. There was no reaction.

The path twisted up ahead and disappeared into the trees. As they took their first step around the curve, Elena and her gang demonstrated their teamwork.

Turning his torso just a bit to the right, Nichou let a streak of black fly from his right hand. The throwing knife he'd hurled with a speed that could only be termed ungodly was swallowed by the trees. It was only seconds later that the barrel of Stahl's gun and the end of Tan's nozzle were brought to bear on the same spot.

And after a few seconds more, Stahl muttered, "It's stopped."

He wasn't talking about the throwing knife. Rather, he meant whatever they could sense following them.

Eyes glittering, Elena said, "Your knife disappeared. Was this a bust?"

"No, we would've heard it if it'd been blocked. And there would've been the sound of it sticking into a tree if it was dodged. But I don't think anything could've caught my blade."

"Then what happened?" Elena asked, not doubting her friend's ability in the least.

"Well, it was probably—," Nichou was saying when a black figure dropped from the sky without a sound. "Head-taker!" he shouted as a hirsute arm wrapped around his neck and he was lifted high into the air.

Before flame could spit from Stahl's firearm, Elena had sent the weighted end of her chain whirring after the creature. There was the crack of bone and an almost beastly howl of pain, and with that Nichou crashed back to earth. The snap of branches continued and something rained down on the group like a mist, then stillness returned.

The sun still hung in the sky. Yet there wasn't the chirping of a single insect or the song a single bird to be heard in the forest.

"Shit! This is freaking blood!" Stahl cursed as his fingers revealed the liquid that'd fallen on his bald pate. "At two hundred, that damn head-taker must've finally gone senile if Elena was able to catch a piece of him with her chain," he chided.

"Hey! Just what's *that* supposed to mean?!" Elena said, glaring firmly at Stahl. She then continued, "Well, since I didn't kill it, it'll probably be back. There's no sign of whatever was following us anymore, either. So let's pull ourselves together already and get going."

Their leader brimmed with determination as she started onward, and the three men couldn't help but grin.

No sooner had they started walking than Nichou said to Tan, "Notice anything about that head-taker just now? About the funny way it was dressed?"

"Nah, I was right underneath you, so I didn't get a good look at it. You mean to tell me it was wearing something?"

"Well, *I* saw it," Nichou replied. "It had on a green shirt and striped pants. That was always old man Geppe's favorite outfit."

Tan fell silent.

A year earlier, ninety-year-old Geppe had ventured into the forest to find a plant called "regression grass" that was said to bring back lost youth. But he was never heard from again. Nichou had lived near the old man's house.

"Then it looks like the head-taker really did get old man Geppe after all," Tan finally said.

Rubbing his neck all the while, Nichou replied, "I saw something else, too. On the arm it had around my throat. The whole thing was pretty hairy, but it had a scar by the fold of its elbow. It was exactly like the one Geppe got splitting wood back when I was maybe four or five years old."

"You mean to tell me that thing . . . *that* was old man Geppe?!" Tan said, his voice thin as a thread.

Nichou shook his head, saying, "It couldn't be. It had a face just like a monkey. There's no way it was Geppe."

"That's enough creepy talk out of the two of you," Stahl suddenly interjected.

But the two bikers didn't look startled by his remark. Rather, their expressions suggested he'd saved them from something, as they said no more.

III

The wall of trees ended as abruptly as the stroke of a knife, and their field of view was suddenly dominated by a bizarrely shaped mountain of rocks. But more than the mound of smooth cube-like rocks that literally looked to have been polished with mechanical precision, it was the area around it that drew the eyes of the group. This was their destination.

"Hey, it ain't here!" Stahl called from the lead.

Everyone quickly gazed in the same direction, finding neither blue moss around the rocks nor anything else but black earth.

"How do you like that! It must've died off," Tan clucked.

Throwing her gaze on the mountain of rocks, Elena said, "That can't be. I saw some just last year—up there!"

Her finger pointed to the summit of the rock pile some sixty feet high, where a patch of blue that could've easily been missed clung to the surface.

Turning around, Stahl asked, "Who's going up after it?"

"Me," Elena replied.

"It's gonna be crazy-dangerous," said Nichou.

"And it'd be any safer for the rest of you?"

Still massaging his neck, Nichou shrugged his shoulders.

"The head-taker might come back. Keep your eyes open."

And leaving them with that, Elena grabbed hold of a nearby outcropping of rock. As she nimbly climbed, a dark gauze seemed to cling to her body. The dusky eve was drawing closer.

Holding his firearm at the ready, Stahl anxiously scanned his surroundings. "The wind's picking up," he said.

"Hell, the wind's gonna be the least of our worries," Tan replied. Looking over at Nichou, he said, "You don't look so hot. You okay?"

Rubbing his neck all the while, Nichou wiped the sweat from his brow with his other hand.

"You know, I heard this story from Mama Kipsch once," Tan said as he adjusted his grip on the metal nozzle of his weapon. "Ages and ages ago, it seems the Nobility used this pile of rocks for certain experiments. That's why it looks all neat and artificial."

"What kind of experiments?" asked Nichou.

"Well, in order to make the monsters they spread all over the Frontier, they needed to collect normal animals first. Breeding stock, I guess you could say. This rock thingy was supposedly a conning tower for that. They say that's how new species like head-takers, toothless suckermouths, and whatnot got made."

"They sure did screw things up for us."

"Hey, you're sounding a little better now, Nichou."

"Yeah, finally," he said, grinning at his friend but never taking his hand away from his neck.

Cupping one hand by the side of his mouth, Stahl shouted toward the sky, "How's it going, Elena?" Of course, he'd watched to make sure Elena had sure footing before he said anything.

"I'm okay. Just a little further to go."

Relieved at her reply, the second-in-command had just turned back toward the woods when a shriek drifted down to him.

Stahl grunted in alarm as he whipped around, and his eyes were met by the sight of Elena with a number of tendrils that could've been vines or ropes wrapped around her body. Spilling down from the very top of the mountain, they clearly showed signs of moving of their own volition.

But it was Elena who'd been really surprised. Just as she was reaching for the moss that clung to the underside of a rock, the things had reached down from above and snared her. Naturally she'd been unnerved and had nearly fallen. But irony still abounded in the world, and it was these very same strange tendrils that'd saved her from that fall. And the second they'd twined around her, Elena had noticed the most surprising thing. They were cold and hard to the touch—metal. This was no living creature.

"Don't shoot, guys!" she shouted down to her gang as she pried off the wriggling tentacles, while her right hand slid down to the cylinder that hung on her belt. It was an incendiary grenade her late father had purchased in the utmost secrecy from a merchant out of the Capital. Once she pulled the pin and threw it, it would char everything within a hundred-fifty-foot radius with ten thousand degrees of heat five seconds later. Or melt it, it this case. Although it was probably crazy of her to use it in this situation, she had no alternative.

Elena grabbed the pin with her teeth. Suddenly, the rest of the grenade was pulled away from her. Clutching the silvery cylinder, a tentacle of the same color was thrashing around just above the girl's head. The sound of the burning fuse was painfully audible.

Four seconds to go.

"Hurry up and take the damn thing already!" the girl shouted.

Cold as the situation made her blood run, it was astonishing she could speak at all. More surprising yet was the fact that she didn't ask her friends below for help.

Of course, even if she had called out to them, there was some question as to whether the three men would've been able to aid her. For just then, the trio had grown tense at the sight of a bizarre figure coming out of the forest.

Its torso was that of a human male, bare-naked and well-muscled—but below that was a long tail that twisted along behind him. Even with him fifteen feet out of the woods, the end was still hidden among the trees, like a snake. The blue-green scales that reflected the evening afterglow covered a lower half writhing as sinuously as a serpent. It actually *was* a snake.

Though the creature had a vacant gaze until it reached the trio, when it halted and slowly appraised the men, its eyes began to blaze with a phosphorescent green.

"You have the ssstink of head-taker blood about you. But you'll be my meal, not hisss!" it declared, its sibilant tone like the air rasping from a punctured tire.

And with that cry, the serpent man suddenly tried to grab Stahl.

A huge black hole opened in its face—right in the middle of its forehead.

Failing to expend all its energy inside the creature's brain, the three-quarter-inch ball of lead Stahl's firearm had sent through the serpent man's brow had burst from the back of the thing's head along with a vast quantity of gray matter. But in less than a second the entrance and exit wounds both closed and the serpent man smirked at the burly biker.

This was the descendant of creatures the Nobility had created, and its ability to regenerate damage was staggering. The expression it wore was no longer that of a human, but rather was the face of a fiend. As its mouth snapped open, a thin ribbon of tongue slid out, the end of which was forked.

A gout of orange blew into the creature's face. Flames. They billowed from the nozzle Tan held. The tank strapped to his back was filled with an oily substance that burned at high temperatures, and when it was discharged by compressed air, the liquid ignited from friction with the atmosphere. In other words, it was a flamethrower.

Apparently this supernatural creature that seemed so inured to being hit or stabbed or even shot couldn't regenerate the damage from burns, for as the flames enveloped it and its skin quickly baked and peeled, its ophidian form began a wild dance in the throes of death.

"I got it!" Elena shouted, but Stahl was the only one who could spare a look up at her.

Elena was coming back down, and the item tucked under her arm was definitely a big chunk of blue moss. Her eyes declared her delight at this accomplishment while flames flickered in their depths.

Just as the girl groaned with the effort of her descent, flames whooshed madly from the rocky summit and the whole mound rattled.

"Hurry up! That thing's ready to collapse!" Stahl shouted to her.

"I know, so get ready to make a catch!"

And once she'd said that, Elena didn't toss down the moss as expected, but rather threw herself into the air.

Not completely prepared, Stahl managed to catch her shapely form but wound up flat on his ass.

"Damn, that hurt," he groaned while Elena promptly got to her feet.

The girl's eyes went wide at the sight of the weird serpent creature writhing before her. Its tail looked to be a good thirty feet long, and in its wild thrashing it struck the ground repeatedly. Every time it did so, the rumble seemed to reach the very heavens.

Suddenly, a mass of rock landed on the creature's tail. Smashing it flat, the boulder went on to bounce once or twice more on the ground.

Fighting desperately to maintain her balance all the while, Elena raced for the woods. Behind her, the mountain—or rather, the rock pyramid—had come tumbling down like a pile of dominos.

"What the hell's going on?" Stahl asked as they made a mad dash for the path that'd brought them there.

"That stupid tentacle grabbed the incendiary grenade from me— with the fuse going—and pulled it back into the rocks. It must be some kind of animal catcher or something. I wonder what it looks like under all those rocks . . ."

"Oh, so you wanna see the Nobles' machines up close, do you?"

"Are you kidding me?!" Elena shot back, and then she heard the undeniable sound of hoofbeats behind them. But why was it the Frontier woman pictured not the Nobility, but rather the Hunter in black?

Turning to look, Elena froze.

The horse seemed to be running in slow motion just to keep pace with her friends as they fled, and on it sat the Black Knight. She'd seen him many times before. And although she found the might of the leader of the four knights as intimidating as always, she had no time for such emotions with him on their tail. He was a veritable grim reaper. But, what would he be doing out here?

"Shit!" cried Tan. He, too, had frozen in his tracks, but he pointed the nozzle of his weapon at the Black Knight. It spat a ball of fire.

Not even trying to avoid it, the Black Knight rode straight into the blast, then through it. The flames slid right across his armor and cape, and then vanished.

A streak of light zipped up from the ground toward the sky. Without so much as a cry of pain, Tan was sliced right down the middle. The iron-shod hooves trampled his body, splitting the brave man into two separate pieces before he fell in the brush.

Elena halted. Turning, she glared at the knight following her. Stahl and Nichou both followed her lead, and the Black Knight stopped at the same time.

"So it's you after all. You've been on our tail ever since we first set foot in the forest, haven't you?" Elena asked in a demanding tone after the flutter in her chest had subsided.

"Indeed I have," he replied, his voice like a rumbling from deep in the earth.

"Why the hell were you following us?"

"The answer should be obvious. I can't have you bringing that moss back to the village. Because then I wouldn't be able to dispose of all those abominations."

"But this will put them right!" Elena cried. "They won't be your kind any more."

"They are filth!"

A beam of light shot out, shattering the ground right in front of Elena. But even as the soil showered her, Elena didn't recoil.

"Hold on just a minute!" the girl shouted, her mouth open as wide as it would go.

Perhaps her bluster actually worked, for the Black Knight stopped moving.

This was a do-or-die situation. With new determination, Elena said, "I'll let you in on a little secret. Something concerning the wonderful princess you've sworn allegiance to."

"Something about the princess?" the Black Knight muttered dubiously, though there was laughter in his voice. Undoubtedly he was convinced this was some fabrication on her part to stall for time.

"That's right, I'm talking about that bitch. Does your precious princess approve of what you're doing?"

The Black Knight said nothing.

"That's what I thought. Honesty is a virtue, you know. But the way you pretend to be all loyal and stuff yet run around disobeying orders behind her back is why she's gonna put you out like so much trash."

"Like trash? Me?" the Black Knight asked, his tone naturally sounding suspicious. These were remarks no one could've imagined coming from this man.

"No, not *just* you—all of you!" Realizing the upper hand was now hers, Elena let her strength flow into her voice as she said, "I'm telling you this as a special favor. Your precious princess actually asked me and D to get rid of the lot of you."

After blurting out the words, Elena was frightened by the response they might bring.

Silence descended, and the beating of the girl's heart rang through her head like a gong.

The shoulders of the Black Knight trembled. A low voice spilled from somewhere in his armor.

She wondered if he was crying. Even Stahl and Nichou looked at each other. But suddenly Elena realized she was mistaken.

The twilight was beaten back by a great booming laugh.

"I never would've thought you'd say such a thing. In all my days, I've never heard anything half so entertaining! So, the princess appointed the two of you to dispose of us, did she?"

"It's true!" Elena snapped back even as realized it was pointless to debate him. The black harbinger of death would surely spread its lethal wings over her head.

Sure enough, the Black Knight began to advance. Not rushing, but slowly. Like a massive mountain.

"From the fight you gave me last night, I felt you had promise despite being human. But when you resort to such tricks, I'm sorely disappointed. What's more, your little ploy couldn't possibly have been more impertinent. It's unforgivable."

"Who are you to talk?! You came sneaking along after us! Why didn't you just show yourself from the very beginning, eh?"

"I wanted to see what you'd do first," the Black Knight replied. "To come out to this forest knowing what time it would be takes a formidable store of determination and strength. And I thought it would be nice to see those traits for myself. I was also curious as to what you'd be searching for."

"When did you start following us?" Elena asked, groping for a question. Now she actually was trying to buy some time. Even if it only kept her alive a few minutes longer, she couldn't miss any chance to improve her odds of delivering the blue moss.

"When you and the others left the village."

"You're a creep. You've been spying on us all along, haven't you?"

"All for the good of the princess," the Black Knight said, his form growing larger by the second.

Elena finally noticed that he was steadily approaching her.

"Run for it, Elena!" Stahl shouted as he suddenly jumped between the two of them. Thunder and flames flew from his gun. A hard thud resounded far off, and the Black Knight's upper body swayed every so slightly. A shallow indentation had been left in the brow of his helm. Around it, other dents formed in rapid succession as bullets and sparks bounced off of him.

"Sorry," Elena said, kicking off the ground with the second shot. The report from Stahl's weapon was like a knife in her heart.

Although she thought about diving between the trees to take the Black Knight's horse out of play, Elena knew that if he reached the bikes before she did, she'd be finished anyway. She ran as fast as her legs would carry her. Then she heard hoofbeats. It felt as if all the blood had drained from her body.

"Stahl," she said, the name coming to her lips naturally.

The beating of the iron-shod hooves had come to within three feet of her, and the hot breath of a horse brushed the nape of her neck.

So, this is the end? she thought for a second, and then a roar to shake the very heavens came from off to the right.

Dance of the Roses

CHAPTER 5

I

Although the cry was one Elena had heard before, she'd never actually seen the thing itself. Known simply as "the forest dweller," it was fabled to bite the heads off fire dragons and use massive trees as toothpicks. And although the biker didn't put much stock in such tales, the colossal bones that were occasionally discovered near the forest made it clear the creature was a danger she'd never want to encounter.

The form that'd just pounced on the Black Knight was roughly ten feet tall, covered with hair and circular in shape. Though it had arms and legs twice as thick as a man could reach around, there was no indication of any fingers or toes. And while Elena figured the smell of the head-taker's blood on her had drawn it here, it was literally a heaven-sent guardian.

Just as the girl was about to make a run for it, she heard a heavy impact and a horse whinnying behind her. She turned to look in spite of herself.

The Black Knight and his steed had both been knocked flat. The forest dweller raised one hand and smashed it down on the horse's belly. Its barding dented, and the horse let out a pained whinny. Then Elena watched as a band of light sank halfway into the thing's woolly shoulder. Black spray rained down on the branches and leaves, staining the twilight.

The forest dweller swung the opposite hand. There was a dull thud as the knight was knocked backward by a remarkable hook.

"He's all yours!" Elena shouted, blowing a kiss at the creature before her feet tore into the ground. Hope had welled within her again, and the exit was right before her eyes. She felt like she could actually hear the sound of her field of view widening.

Elena trembled. Her bike was right where she'd left it and in exactly the same shape. Climbing onto it, she hit the starter. The engine growled.

"Elena!"

The girl thought she'd imagined someone calling her name. And then she heard it again—very close to her. Before she could get its precise location, a figure came running toward her.

"Nichou—"

"I managed to get away. Stahl told me to look after you."

"Was he—?"

"Yeah, he bought it," Nichou said, holding his neck.

Feeling her tears building, Elena turned her face away. "Mount up. Let's go," she said.

"No, not yet."

"Huh?"

Nichou's face was horribly warped. "Watch this, Elena," he said.

Putting his hands to either side of his head, he lifted it right up. It came off so easily, Elena was even less surprised than she would've expected.

"Nichou—"

The ground rumbled roughly as the figure that sprang from the forest came down about fifteen feet from the two of them. With arms and legs covered with black bristles, it was obviously the head-taker. Elena wasn't even surprised to see that it wore a shirt and pants.

As the girl watched the deep red blood spouting up from Nichou, her hand instinctively went for the chain around her waist.

The slight forward hunch of the creature was somewhat ape-like— that must've been what it'd been in the beginning. Treading its way across the grass, the head-taker stopped behind Nichou, extended both hands, and took the head the decapitated biker was holding up. It then casually tossed it.

The head-taker reached for its own head.

"You must be joking," Elena muttered, her body stiffened by a fearful premonition.

Pulling its own head off, the head-taker set it down on Nichou's neck—which was still spouting blood. The head was pointing the wrong way. But with a sick grinding sound it twisted around to face Elena. At the very same time, the head-taker's body slumped to the ground. That great simian face with its sloping brow and strangely prognathous jaw then bared its fangs at the girl.

By swapping heads, it had effectively transplanted its brain. In this manner, the head-taker could replace its aging body and essentially live forever.

The creature's mouth snapped open viciously. Every last tooth lining the top and bottom of its crimson maw was as sharp as a needle.

Nichou's body leapt into the air. Just as it was about to land on her, Elena moved out of reflex. And her bike was already running.

It seemed that her vehicle hit the lower half of the creature. Flipping over Elena's head, the head-taker fell into the bushes.

Executing a quick turn, Elena flashed her headlight onto Nichou's body. The way his hands came up to shield his eyes was exactly what the head-taker would do.

"This is payback for Nichou!" she shouted.

The laser stabbed through the darkness, searing the palms of the head-taker's hands. Screeching, it took to the air, but there were no branches or trunks to which it might cling.

If she allowed this thing to live, it would claim other victims. She sped toward where it landed.

Her foe was in a crouch. Elena slammed into it at ninety miles per hour.

Nailed it! she thought, but just as all the tension was leaving her body, her bike tilted forward. The vehicle bounded wildly before it fell over with only the whine of its engine still echoing, and it was then that the head-taker stood up straight again. It hurled the wheel it held in its right hand at the bike. Elena lay by the vehicle. The wheel landed near her feet, and then toppled over.

It was her motorcycle's front wheel. Though it'd been secured by steel bolts, the head-taker had managed to tear it off with a swipe of one hand.

Whether the gagging sound that escaped the creature now was simply its breathing or the sound of its laughter was impossible to say. As it lumbered over to Elena, the expression it wore bore hints of malice, hunger and an unmistakable lust. Elena had landed on her back, and due to her struggles, the front of her top had been ripped wide, leaving her pale breasts half exposed, while a diagonal slash down the right thigh of her pants yawned to reveal more of her sweet, nubile flesh. After leering down at her exposed portions and noting the full lines of her bosom, the head-taker licked its lips. Both its hands grabbed her breasts through her shirt.

Elena didn't move a muscle.

Surely the beast with a human body had something in mind as it clambered on top of Elena. The stage now set for its depraved acts there in the moonlight, the creature's monstrous mouth was about to close on Elena's half-open lips when there was an unearthly howl and the head-taker's upper body bent backward. The creature braced its legs in an attempt to flee, but the arm wrapped around its waist wouldn't allow that.

"Too bad. I've been falling off bikes all my life, so I'm used to it," Elena sneered, her left arm locked on her foe's waist while her right hand gouged his flank with a weapon. "This little throwing knife belonged to Nichou, who you killed. A long time ago, he gave it to me as a memento. So just consider this a stab from him!"

After she'd plunged the weapon into the hard, wriggling torso three times, it ceased to struggle. Elena no longer held the body as it now slowly toppled backward, allowing the girl to quickly get to her feet. Every inch of her ached. No matter how accustomed to spills she might be, being thrown from her bike at ninety miles per hour still left her body screaming in a dozen places. And as she turned to head back to where Stahl and the others had left their bikes, Elena found there was one important point she'd overlooked.

Not ten feet from her stood the Black Knight.

"How long have you been watching?" she asked as she checked on the moss she'd shoved into her shirt pocket. Her legs felt like they were about to melt.

"You did splendidly," the Black Knight said in a calm voice.

But Elena wasn't in any shape to take that as a compliment.

"There's nothing lower than a man who'd just stand around watching a woman bust her ass. Drop dead!"

Elena gauged the distance to the other bikes. Twelve feet. Not far at all.

The Black Knight simply remained there in the dark, and then spoke. Elena couldn't understand it.

What did he just say? Come with me?

"Hyah!" Elena cried as the end of her chain flew from her right hand. The blow had all her might behind it, but the Black Knight easily batted it down with his left hand. Her arms numbed by the shock of that impact, Elena dropped the chain.

I suppose this is the end, she thought.

The darkness spread before her eyes. The last sight she saw was the Black Knight as he closed on her.

I'm sorry, Stahl, Tan, Nichou . . . Looks like I've had it, too.

The girl regained consciousness. From the way she came to her senses so quickly, not long had passed since she'd collapsed. She was lying in some brush.

As Elena started to get up, her every hair stood on end. An ineffable lust for killing whirled through the darkened space.

There was a moon out. Beneath it, a pair of figures appeared to be facing each other. To the right was the Black Knight. The night winds that made the grass on the plains sway caused the coat of the figure on the left to flutter gracefully.

"D," Elena said, sounding more dazed than thrilled.

The Black Knight backed away unexpectedly, saying, "I believe I shall call it a night here."

"I won't," D replied.

Pointing to Elena, the Black Knight said, "It'll take time to defeat me, even for you. And that girl will likely die in the meantime. Of course, if she has no connection to you, that won't matter much, but a woman of her caliber deserves better than to die pitifully out in the wilderness."

Without waiting for D's reply, the knight walked off toward the woods. His black charger awaited him. Apparently it'd weathered the attack by the forest dweller.

D came over to the woman.

Turning her face away, Elena said, "I'm sorry. I've gone and got in your way. If this hadn't happened to me, you'd have killed him just now."

D's left hand came to rest on her forehead. Elena turned and looked at D in spite of herself. Her pain had suddenly faded. Their eyes met. Feeling as if the sheer depth of the Hunter's eyes would swallow her, Elena was actually scared and tried her best to shut her eyelids.

D backed away from her. He didn't tell her to get up, or ask if she could stand. He didn't even offer to help her.

Elena got up on her own.

"What are you doing out here?" she asked, wondering if he'd say he was worried and came to check up on her.

"I was teleported from the castle all the way to the border. I was just on my way back."

That's about as short and sweet as can be, she thought. That was just like him, too.

The two of them started over to his horse and her bike.

"So, aren't you even gonna ask me what I'm doing out here?" Elena said, voicing all the discontent that filled her heart.

Naturally, there was no reply.

Although she tried to restrain it, the girl let a sigh escape.

"You really don't give a rat's ass about me, do you? I suppose I did take it upon myself to go up to the castle, after all. But for what it's worth, we've fought on the same side, you know. It'd be nice if you'd at least ask me if I was okay or tell me I did a good job or something," she said, not aloud, but in her heart of hearts.

D straddled his steed. The cyborg horse was one he'd acquired from a farmer on the way back, as was the sword he now wore. Elena got on Stahl's bike. When she started its engine, D turned to her and said, "Were your friends killed?"

"Yeah. And I'm the one who invited them out here," Elena replied, shutting her eyes. How was she going to tell their families?

For a heartbeat she was sure he'd say something to console her now, but D galloped off in a gust of wind, as if to leave the girl alone with her bitter sentiments.

II

The gates to the village were shut, and shouts arose from inside. The cries came from both men and women. And it sounded like the angry bellows were exceeded by the wails of pain.

"Open up!" the girl cried, but there was no response.

Something was going on. It was easy enough to imagine what that could be, but Elena tried her best to keep such thoughts from flooding her consciousness. Her heart was horribly cold.

The gates were over ten feet tall. As the girl stood there powerless, an arm like steel wrapped around her waist. But her cry of astonishment wasn't prompted by its grasp, but because she then went sailing high over the gate. Even their landing was quiet.

"The square's over that way, isn't it?" asked D.

For those who didn't know the power that lurked in the blood of a dhampir, his leap would've been unbelievable.

"That's right!" Elena cried.

Her head was killing her—it pounded with the excitement that always spilled from hope. On the way back to the village, she'd told the Hunter about what had transpired the night before. Although she had no problem with his lack of reaction, she had to wonder if her tale had done the trick.

There was no sign of anyone on the streets. But as the pair approached the square, the shouting grew louder.

Turning the corner, Elena had the wind knocked out of her.

The tent was ablaze. The flames burnt their image into her eyes. Around the fire, mobs of villagers lingered with the four hues of roses blooming from their bodies. The form of a knight raced by them, and a long, straight shaft pierced the chests of the villagers at an angle. Killed instantly, they were easily lifted on the lance with one hand before the knight then cast their bodies into the flames.

"The Blue Knight," Elena growled, feeling every drop of blood in her body come to a boil. She even forgot all about D.

Near the tent, the people still milling around were outnumbered by those now heaped motionless on the ground by several to one. Occasionally there was the crack of a gunshot, and the Blue Knight would reel as sparks danced on his chest or abdomen. His charger would then race to the shooter with incredible speed, and the perpetrator would loose their dying screams from the end of the knight's lance.

Someone shouted at him to stop.

A child could be heard crying out for his father.

"That lousy murderer . . . ," Elena muttered, and she was just about to dash forward when a black shape passed her.

As the man in the long coat headed toward the flames, he looked like some gorgeous idol of a god of war trimmed in crimson lotus blossoms.

Engaged in butchery some forty feet ahead of the young man, the blue figure whirled around on his steed as if he'd been struck by a bolt of unseen lightning.

"Where have you been?" he asked with pleasure when he saw D. "I came down here because the Black Knight told me to dispose of these scum, but my heart was actually set on doing battle with you. I've already killed forty or fifty of them. Are you going to try and stop me, D?"

"That's my job," D replied as his blade whined from the sheath on his back.

The Blue Knight adjusted his grip on his lance.

Both the hues and the crackling of the raging flames seemed to freeze solid from the lethal intent that billowed between the two men.

D sprinted; his sword streamed along behind him. As the blade painted a silvery arc aimed at the legs of the horse, the blue mount and rider leapt toward the moon. The knight's lance was aimed by turns at D's chest and his back. While he held but a single weapon, it looked for all the world like he had two.

Blocking both thrusts, D made a leap and blocked the second blow in midair. Surely, even the Blue Knight had never considered the possibility of anyone human coming at him from above while he was galloping along on his horse.

As the end of D's blade was coming down, it suddenly changed direction. The sword swung to the right in a parrying blow, and was assailed by a horizontal arc of black. The Blue Knight had brought a second lance holstered on his horse's flank into play.

D's blade shattered, and the Hunter was thrown through the air. Amid the flames, his coat danced like nightmare-shrouded wings.

A split second lay between life and death. As Elena watched the flying Hunter, her brain burned with a feeling that was almost rapture.

This was precisely the moment the Blue Knight had been waiting for. In midair, no target whatsoever would be able to avoid his lance. At least, so long as it was human.

With ample time to take aim, the Blue Knight hurled his weapon. And his aim was true—run through from the belly to the back, D tumbled head over heels to the ground.

Reining his steed to a halt, the Blue Knight adjusted his grip on his remaining lance. Thirty feet from him, D was down on one knee.

"Now it ends. Wait for me in the hereafter, D!"

With the thunder of iron-shod hooves, the steely knight charged. But before the rider could ever bring his lance to bear, D would surely be trampled beneath the hooves of his steed. As the Blue

Knight swung his weapon around, he never took his eyes off his target for an instant. But he couldn't believe what he saw. Still impaled on the other lance, the young man in black rose steadily to his feet. The knight's exclamation was louder than even the roar of hooves pounding the earth, but was it a cry of surprise or a grunt of deadly determination?

Just as the rider passed the man, there was a sharp sound and a lance went sailing into the air. Wheeling his horse around in front of one of the locals' houses with the skill of an expert horseman, the Blue Knight was about to embark on another attack when he was dumbstruck. There was no lance in his hands. The instant he noticed this, D appeared before him like some guardian demon with the very same lance that'd previously impaled him in his right hand. The weapon in question scorched through the air to punch through both the knight's armor and his chest.

"You did it, D! You really did it!" Elena shouted.

But her jubilant cries were cut short by the sound of hoofbeats. Incredibly, the horse had started to gallop off still bearing the Blue Knight, who'd clearly been pierced right through the heart.

"Stop that thing!" someone shouted.

"Don't let it get back to the castle!" cried another villager who'd apparently seen what'd happened and feared the princess's retribution.

With poles and spade-like implements they struck at the beast, but the horse shrugged off the blows and dashed toward the rear gate to the village.

"D!" Elena exclaimed as she made a single-minded dash for him. But the Vampire Hunter simply adjusted the brim of his traveler's hat as if nothing at all had transpired. "You got run through . . . Are you hurt bad?"

Seeing his bloodstained abdomen, Elena shuddered for the first time at the thought of what this gorgeous young man was.

"Seems we've got a hell of a man in town now," said a hoarse female voice. Mama Kipsch. "The first time I laid eyes on you, I thought you were far too pretty," she continued. "And now that I see how fast you heal—I'd say you're a dhampir, aren't you?"

"That's right," the Hunter replied.

Elena was speechless.

"No second-rate warrior would ever think of getting their opponent's lance to replace their own broken sword. And seeing where you let yourself be impaled to do so, I don't suppose you're an average dhampir, either. You did say your name was D, didn't you?" the old woman asked, staring at him with glittering eyes.

"That's right," D again replied softly.

Shifting her gaze from him, Mama Kipsch turned to the tent where the flames were almost under control and saw the corpses littering the area. "From the very start, those fiends never intended to let *all of us* get through this, I'd say. But using that moss you've got poking out of your pocket, we'll have everyone back to normal in two or three days. Elena, you'd best come back to my place tonight."

"I'll help out any way I can, Mama Kipsch."

"That's not quite what I was talking about," the crone said, her wise old eyes narrowing sorrowfully. "The real thing we have to worry about is what the people who've been put through all this will do, you see." Turning to D, she said, "I'm sure you'd know all about that."

The leisurely nod of the Hunter seemed to satisfy the old woman.

"In that case, you'd best stick close to this girl," she told him. "The real trouble will start once the sun begins to shower its blessings on us again."

Mama Kipsch's prediction was right on the mark. The next day, every villager who'd been spared the Noble transformation came storming out to the witch doctor's house to find Elena. As Elena snorted that she'd go out and give them a piece of her mind, Mama Kipsch physically stopped her and tried to talk to them in her place. However, she made no progress, and the crowd remained emphatic that she send Elena out, until the biker finally appeared in the doorway.

"This is your fault! All of it!" shouted the leader of the pack—Gary, the guard from the tent. "Yeah, all because of you and that young feller! Send him on out, too!"

"He's not here," Elena shot back, and a pain spread through her heart—D had ignored her and gone back to village outskirts. "But, don't you get it yet? He's the only one who can destroy those bastards. His strength will free us from the oppression of the Nobility!"

"Who in the world asked him to do that?" one of the women shouted.

That was the very question Elena had dreaded.

"We've had it pretty good so far, haven't we? We've always managed to coexist somehow with the princess up in the castle and her knights, right? Sure, there's been some ugliness. But if we just grit our teeth through it, there's always peace again later, isn't there? There's a hell of a lot more ugliness in this world we live in. We're *lucky* we don't have to see most of it."

"Sure, just as long as we obey all their rules," Elena snapped back. "We can't leave the village now. They carry off husbands and wives, children and lovers, and we can't say a thing about it. What the hell is so lucky about a life where all our loved ones can be taken away on one of their whims?!"

"Well, people die from famine or fires all the time," someone else cried out. "They're just like that—a natural calamity us mortals can't do a thing about. Come what may, we've got no choice but to just keep our heads bowed and our voices low, right? When you think of it—"

"You talk like a fucking slave!" Elena groaned in the bottom of her throat as the weighted end of her chain whistled out.

Although she shouldn't have been able to see him very well from her location, the man who flipped backward with a cry of pain was the very same person who'd just been talking. His nose was now broken.

The crowd backed away, leaving a semicircular clearing just in front of the door.

As Elena hauled back on her chain for another blow, Mama Kipsch caught hold of her arm. "Stop it," the old woman told her. "Don't do anything more to distance them."

"I knew that crazy bitch would show her true colors!" Gary the tent guard howled. "As far as we're concerned, we're in a lot more danger from you down here in the village than we are from the Noble in the castle. Hey, take a good look at this!"

The crowd split down the middle, leaving a single figure between Elena and the others.

Seeing the feeble individual crawling across the ground, Elena exclaimed, "McCay!"

It was one of her compatriots.

"Take a good look at him. He was one of last night's survivors," Gary said with revulsion. "But his right shoulder is broken, his left ear's been torn off, and his left eye popped. And I think you know who did all that."

Elena stood stunned, as if she'd just been struck by lightning.

Her rose-cursed compatriot had one hand raised to ward off the sunlight as he writhed on the ground. But his fingers were all bent in impossible directions.

"You did this. Back in the tent, you beat the shit out of one of your own. Yeah, you talk a good game, but when someone winds up one of the Nobility, you don't know a friend from a piece of garbage. There are others that made it through the night, but they're all beat to hell thanks to you. So before you go acting like you're something special, take a good, hard look at what you've done. And he's not the only one who's been through hell. Just how do you and that young feller plan on taking responsibility for the forty people who died?"

It was a heartbeat later that the *coup de grace* was delivered to the dazed and speechless Elena.

"Give me back my Yohan!" a matronly voice cried. It was that of Mrs. Kaiser, a woman who'd often given Elena milk when she was young. "They killed him yesterday. You used to bounce my son on your knee. Oh, he was only eight years old!"

"I lost my Frida, too," said old Mr. Bangs, who kept a herd of cows on the outskirts of the village. Frida was the same age as Elena, and she'd been an excellent seamstress.

"I just want my Chauve!"

"Give back Pelt!"

Elena covered her ears. She didn't even have Stahl or Nichou or Tan there anymore. McCay writhed at her feet. She wished she were a million miles away, and a keen longing for the forest or the plains of the previous night came over her.

"Give 'er what she's got coming!" someone shouted, but to the girl, the cry seemed to reverberate in another world.

"Throw her in the stocks on the edge of town. Better yet, leave her chained out by the castle for three days and nights!"

As one, the villagers grunted their approval. In that instant, the group became a bloodthirsty mob.

Elena didn't have the strength left to stop the people with bloodshot eyes bearing down on her in a crushing wave. But a single bolt of lightning did it in her place. It'd skimmed by the end of the lead vengeance seeker's nose and imbedded itself in the black soil. The man gasped in terror and the mob halted its advance.

The bolt of lightning had become a blue lance. But the reason the people remained paralyzed like lambs before a two-headed wolf wasn't because they recognized it as the weapon the Blue Knight had left in town. Rather, they'd been frozen by the whistle of it dropping from the sky and the thunder of it sinking into the earth. Not a single one of them dared to turn in the direction from which it'd flown. The crowd froze there in the swelling sunlight as they listened to the approaching hoofbeats.

"I just knew he'd come," said Mama Kipsch.

At last, the people turned and saw the gorgeous young man on the horse. Before him on the saddle sat a boy of about five, while a burly man with gray hairs scattered among the black stood beside the mount.

"Blasko!"

"And that's his boy Cusca up on the horse. What are they doing with . . ."

"They're here because I had need of a blacksmith," said D.

This was the first time the villagers had ever heard D's voice. The cheeks of every last woman flushed, while the men grew dazed and even enthralled.

Glancing up at D out of the corner of his eye, Blasko the smith said, "When I heard you'd all headed off to string up Elena, I was gonna come out here and stop you. But then this fella came by—" Swallowing hard, the smith continued, "My boy had one of those roses blooming out of him, too. But drinking the medicine Mama Kipsch whipped up last night cured him. Just look at him—sure, he's still got a little trouble with the sun, but at least we don't have to keep him shut away in darkness. I'm sure some of your kin have been saved, too. This feller told me what happened. It seems it was Elena who went out and got the blue moss to make that medicine. So don't go doing anything crazy."

"He's making you say all that," someone in the mob sneered, shaking his fist.

"Nothing doing. All he said was that Elena got the moss. I came here of my own free will. There's no way you can seriously believe deep down in your hearts that the Noble's way is the best. Elena only says what all of us think."

"And I say that's more trouble than we need. We'd be better off without Elena or that guy. When the night comes, the Nobility will retaliate. What the hell are we supposed to do then?!"

"Me and him will protect you," Elena declared as she pointed at D.

"What good will the two of you do?"

"It's not just the two of us," said the girl. "All of you are gonna have to fight, too."

"Don't make me laugh!" the man snarled back at her in the most passionate burst of anger so far. "I'm sure you know just how powerful those four knights are, and they ain't even Nobility! The real sorceress is up in the castle. If things get ugly, she'll come down for us. And when that happens, a lousy stake of wood ain't gonna do us a whole lot of good!"

"He'll take care of the bitch in the castle for us. He's a professional Vampire Hunter. If the knights come into town, the rest of us will have to kill them."

Anxious chatter rolled through the crowd like a wind.

Before the murmur died out, the young man on the horse said in a voice heavy with rust, "All three of the girl's friends were killed. Her right shoulder is dislocated, and she's got a crack in her left femur. She's also got countless minor injuries. Yet she still went and got the moss and fought her way back. Isn't that enough?"

The crowd fell silent.

D continued, "I'll be heading up to the castle soon. And if things don't work out today, I'll go up there again tomorrow. That's my job."

And saying that, the Hunter slowly rode away without anyone shouting at him to stop. The blacksmith and his son went with him.

The villagers looked at each other. Although some of them still muttered misgivings, they'd been robbed of the strength to veto the plan.

Nevertheless, someone said, "Okay, we'll let this go for today. But if the village loses even one more person, Elena, there's gonna be hell to pay. You remember that!"

"I know! I know!" Elena replied, although it sounded more like the words were directed at herself.

The members of crowd sluggishly turned around, then wasted little time in breaking into smaller groups as they dispersed, but Elena alone remained with her eyes aimed in the same direction as ever. That was the way the gorgeous young man had gone, seeming to glow in the sunlight yet, at the same time, like a chunk of ice that sucked the heat out of everything.

"D," the biker tough mumbled as the first fat tear in many years welled in her eye and traced a glistening track down her cheek.

III

Breathtaking sunlight poured through a rainbow of stained glass in the vast chamber. Where the entrance to this room was located remained a mystery—all four walls were solid stone. Aside from the figure who stood in its very center, the room was bare of tables or chairs or anything else—an area so antiseptic, it seemed unlikely even a mote of dust lay there.

The figure stood looking straight ahead like a sculpted temple guardian, completely absorbed in his thoughts since the previous night, like a lifeless suit of armor.

"What is it, Sir Black Knight?" asked the crimson form who'd appeared from somewhere, though neither the walls nor the floor showed any sign of having opened. "You've been like this for a good five hours now. What holds your thoughts?"

The Red Knight's query received no reply.

"If it's the Blue Knight, what happened was unavoidable. While the princess may be angry, what we've done is absolutely correct. That's what he died for. And I'm sure that's exactly how he would've wanted it."

"No, that's not it," the black sculpture replied. Low as his voice was, it echoed through the chamber nonetheless.

"What then?"

"It's the princess that concerns me."

"Oh."

"I wonder just how our princess will take the death of the Blue Knight."

"Really? That isn't like you at all. Whether we live or die is of no concern to the princess, and you of all people shouldn't need me to remind you of that. We only live to protect the princess and her castle, and to deliver her edicts to the worms below and see that they are carried out, do we not?"

"But do we really live?" the Black Knight said, seeming to heave a sigh.

His words took the Red Knight's breath away.

"Did you happen to see the look the Blue Knight wore on his face in death?" asked the Red Knight.

Just before dawn, their comrade in blue had returned home impaled on his own lance. As the princess was already in repose and the appearance of the White Knight would only complicate matters, the Red Knight had summoned servants from the drifting fog of particles and had them see to everything, while the Black Knight had taken one look at the remains before quickly going back into the manor.

Over the centuries, he had never uttered a single compliment no matter what kind of action had been displayed, and such seemed fitting for a battle-hardened veteran. Therefore, the Red Knight didn't pity the dead man, but rather admired what the Black Knight had done. As he spoke now, it was with all due respect toward his compatriot.

"I took off his helmet. He looked so proud. It was literally the face of a man who'd given his all and battled to the very last. Undoubtedly the battle itself was equally grand. His opponent—"

"It was D, wasn't it?"

"Precisely," the Red Knight said with a nod. The swords on his back clattered together.

"A satisfying death, was it?" the Black Knight muttered, and though the Red Knight tried to comprehend what sentiments might've prompted the remark, he had little luck. "How long has it been since you became one of the four?" the Black Knight asked, his face turned toward the ceiling as if seeking the light.

"Roughly a hundred and fifty years, sir."

"I've lived three times that. And having lived that long, one grows a bit weary."

"I see."

"But now," the Black Knight continued, "I truly feel full of life. I'm actually glad."

"You mean, because we've lost the Blue Knight?"

"Dolt. For the very same reason as yourself, for one thing."

Beneath his helm, the Red Knight grinned. "That could only be D, then."

"At long last, I've met a man who makes me feel in the bottom of my soul that he may well be more than I can handle. It's been so long, Red Knight. For ages and ages I've searched for just such a man."

"Truly—this is an opponent worth gambling our lives against," the Red Knight said, showering their foe with heartfelt praise before holding his tongue for a moment. When he spoke again, it was to say, "But Sir Black Knight—it almost sounds as if you were choosing a time and place to die."

The Black Knight laughed aloud. The same grand laugh as always, it served to ease the apprehension that filled the bosom of the Red Knight. "We have the princess to protect. Though the manor may be a shambles, so long as she remains, our swords and lances must stand ready to pierce her foes. In other words, we shall see to it that D dies for certain. No matter what."

The Red Knight nodded an acknowledgment, but he didn't reply. Battle was a religion to his compatriot.

"Take out your sword," the Black Knight commanded.

Although the order came out of the blue, every inch of the Red Knight surged with vitality. He backed away a few steps. But even as he did so, the heavy armor he wore didn't make a sound.

Before drawing his sword, he asked, "What other reason do you have for being so happy, Sir Black Knight?"

Giving no reply, the Black Knight stepped forward.

When the Red Knight heard a great *whoosh!*, his body went into action. Drawn just in the nick of time, the Red Knight's blade transmitted a terrific shock up his arms as he barely managed to strike out to one side, carving an arc to his right. His hands and feet came into the ideal position.

For an instant, a true killing lust hung in the space between the two of them.

The Black Knight was in the same relaxed pose as always.

The Red Knight was poised to draw another blade from his back with his left hand. The first sword he'd drawn lay on the floor.

The atmosphere suddenly cleared.

"As you've taken your favorite stance, there's not a thing I can do to you now," the Black Knight said, rolling his head from side to side.

"I might well say the same. I'm not certain whether I could've drawn in time to meet a second blow from you, sir," said the Red Knight, and the words came from the very bottom of his heart.

At just that moment, a haughty laugh echoed from nowhere in particular to surround the pair.

"Princess!" the knights exclaimed in amazement, both taking a knee in perfect unison. The light from the dazzling human form before them etched their shadows on the far wall.

"As skillful as ever, I see," the princess's voice remarked. But was it actually the supposedly slumbering princess that spoke, or was this the work of some Noble machinery beyond the ken of even her knights?

"Please forgive our unseemly display," the Black Knight said gravely.

"You've taken it upon yourself to do something rather interesting, my Black Knight."

"Begging your pardon?"

"Don't play coy with me. Last night, you and the Blue Knight ran amok down in the village, did you not? Why, it seems you were trying to destroy all the humans I'd gone to the trouble of blessing with my flowers. Wasn't that a bit presumptuous on your part?"

The Black Knight had no reply.

"I would assume you're prepared to accept your punishment?"

"I believe I am. But—"

"Oh, my! I don't believe anyone has ever used that word with me before. Whatever could it mean?"

Once more at a loss for words, the Black Knight remained silent. Even as an illusion projected in the daylight, the lovely princess remained an absolute, godlike being as far as he was concerned.

He was no Noble. He wasn't even a human enslaved by their bite. If he had to be labeled as anything, then he was a bio-man—a human re-engineered by the Nobility's science for extreme longevity. But, that wasn't necessarily what made him their subordinate. The way the Nobility inspired a kind of voluntary subservience in humans was an ideal topic for psychologists to research. Why were there people who served the Nobility without ever being bitten by them? Though no conclusion had been reached, the most vivid example of that behavior was currently being played out between the princess and her Black Knight.

"The Blue Knight has been slain. Now you yourself must assume the same risk," the shimmering princess said with a tilt of her glowing head. "Oh, I know! I'd like to see you do battle with the White Knight now," she said.

At that, the Red Knight looked up at her, and then desperately lowered his gaze once more.

The Black Knight solemnly replied, "Understood."

"As a matter of fact, I've already summoned him. Come out, please," she said, turning matter-of-factly to where the white figure appeared like a ghost. "Here is your opponent," the illusion of the princess said as she indicated the Black Knight. "Have at him until I call for you to stop. And you're to hold nothing back. As for you, Black Knight—you aren't to use your weapon. You shall battle him empty-handed."

"But that's—," the Red Knight began to say, his head bobbing up in amazement.

"Silence!" the princess snapped, her rebuke shaking the very light that poured through the stained glass.

The Wraith Knights

CHAPTER 6

I

B lasko the smith stared intently at the gleaming blue tip of the lance—he'd just put it under a particle spectroscope for analysis. This was the very same weapon that had stopped the mob in its tracks a bit earlier.

"So you say you want a sword just like this, eh?" said the blacksmith, his consternation and diffidence quite apparent both in his voice and on his face. "What you've got here is molybdenum, chromium steel, an iron polymer, plus some synthetic substance I don't have a clue about—and that's the secret of its cutting strength. Come with me," the man said to D.

They'd arrived straightaway after saving Elena, and less than thirty minutes had elapsed since the incident. The blacksmith was about to walk away, but he stumbled to the ground where he was—as he was taking the lance from the spectroscope, he'd completely forgotten about its weight. And though this oversight was caused by his desperate urge to escape D's exquisite countenance, the smith would've died before admitting as much.

Walking over without a word, D effortlessly lifted the lance.

"That thing's mind-boggling! It must weigh a hundred pounds or more. Something like that could stop a fire dragon, or even a kraken."

Rubbing his left arm all the while, the blacksmith led D around to his backyard.

Needless to say, D had requested that Blasko craft a sword that could penetrate the knights' armor. While the Hunter was skillful enough to deal each of them a fatal blow even with a lesser blade, his opponents were also superhuman. It was entirely possible they might parry his blow or make him miss a vital spot. And if his sword were to break every time that happened, even the great D would be left powerless.

"What do you think?" the smith said with pride as they surveyed his garden.

"My, oh, my!" a voice exclaimed behind him.

Seeming satisfied with the appreciative remark, the smith took another step or two before the hoarseness of that same voice struck him as peculiar and he turned around. Quickly shaking his head with a quizzical expression, he then coolly strutted out into the middle of the garden.

Blasko certainly had every reason to be proud of his yard. The grass and black soil were crowded with rows of stone sculptures and metal castings that certainly looked to be the work of the Nobility. A hero of antiquity with sword in hand, a giant cyclops, a mermaid strumming a lyre, a hundred-legged spider from the stratosphere, the wildly cavorting Pan playing his flute, and on and on—some of the statues were life-size, but others were more than thirty feet tall. Since some of those colossal pieces were busts, the blacksmith's garden seemed more like an enchanted arbor that left his guests feeling like they'd stepped into some avant-garde art museum in the Capital. And scattered among the statues were Noble coffins that were undoubtedly the genuine article.

"I don't suppose it matters much which we use. But how about we try this?" the smith said as he indicated a black globe that lay on the grass. It alone seemed to have nothing whatsoever to do with the world of art. The globe was approximately three feet in diameter, and there wasn't a single gleam or reflection on it, as if it were merely sucking up all the sunlight that touched it.

"All of this is stuff I picked up from a merchant who specializes in garden ornaments from the Nobles' ruins. Not that I sit around admiring them or anything," Blasko added. "You see, they're all here so I can test my handiwork on them."

Now that he mentioned it, every statue was marked with deep gouges or fine cracks, and some of them even had parts sliced clean off.

"You can't go wrong with the stuff the Nobility made," the blacksmith continued. "It's a hundred times tougher than the crummy armor and helms you run into, but even then, there hasn't been anything my blades haven't been able to cut. Except for that one sphere there, that is. Gave it holy hell with some of the Nobility's weapons, too, but the results were the same. What I'd like to see is what the point of that lance can do. Would you give it here for a second?" he asked.

A true professional, Blasko was so well-braced as he took the lance from D's hand that only the word "splendid" could do him justice. His lower body didn't show the slightest danger of buckling under the load now.

"Take that!" he cried, putting more than enough resolve into a thrust at the center of the sphere.

But without so much as a spark the lance bounced off, and as the smith took a hard spill on his tail, the weapon came whistling down at him.

"Holy—," Blasko groaned, but the tip of the lance stopped right before his painfully wide eyes.

Pulling the lance away with the same left hand that'd caught it, D eyed the sphere.

"From the way that felt, it's no use. Don't bother," the smith said with a dismissive wave of his hands as he sat there on his rump. But when he saw how easily D held the weapon in his left hand, his face went pale.

Not seeming to make any real effort, D simply swept out with his hand.

The blacksmith stared incredulously at the sphere as the lance jutted from the heart of it. Looking at D, he asked, "Can you pull it out?"

After the Hunter easily drew it from the sphere, the smith ran his fingers almost lovingly over the tip. With a sullen face he said, "A hell of a thing, that is. I still doubt if I can even do this."

"How many days to make a sword from it?" asked D.

"Three, working day and night."

"Have it for me tomorrow night."

"Good enough," the blacksmith replied. "Not because I'm crazy about this weapon, but because I can't get over your skill. I'll craft it for you, but it'll be no ordinary sword. What's your name, anyway?"

"D," the Hunter replied.

The blacksmith nodded. His eyes were sparkling.

"It'll be an honor. I'll get to go to my grave as the smith who forged D's sword."

It wasn't long after that D returned to his camp in the ruins. Elena was leaning back against one of the stone columns. A bike was parked close-by. Seeing D, she raised one hand and said, "Hey there, stranger!"

Her other shoulder was wrapped in bandages.

"Go home," D said curtly.

"No way. There's no one there, and Stahl's folks will just force their way in. When I went by earlier to pay my respects, they stabbed me," the girl said, and as she lightly brushed her bandages, they darkened slightly with blood. "And it's not like anyone else is much happier with me. But relax. I'm not gonna ask you to let me stay with you or anything stupid like that. The fact is, I came out here before I even knew what I was doing. But I'll be going soon."

Tethering his horse's reins, D took a bundle off the animal's back.

"What's the story with those swords?" asked the girl.

"Our friends will be coming out again tonight. I can't fight them without weapons."

The Hunter had borrowed the swords from the blacksmith. Although he had ten in all, none of them would last more than a single blow.

"Hey, let me fight, too! Alongside you," Elena said in a forceful tone.

"The only reason you're still alive is because the Black Knight went easy on you."

"I know that. That's why I wanna fight with you. On my own, I couldn't so much as scratch the Nobles' armor. But with you, I think we could get something done. After all, if they don't kill me, the folks in the village probably will. So if I'm gonna go out, I wanna at least hurt those bastards some."

"You're rather tenacious, aren't you?" D remarked.

"You got that right. See, I've gotta pay them back for *this*," Elena said, grabbing her shirt with both hands and pulling it wide open.

She didn't have anything on underneath it. Below the ample curve of her breasts, a pair of deep red lines formed an "x" that covered her whole belly. The wounds had clearly been left by a sword.

"When I was five, that bitch attacked my house. And that's when she got my father and mother, and my little brother and sister, though they didn't really die until the next day, when the mayor hammered stakes into the four of them. The little ones were only two and four. The princess had the White Knight with her, and he carved this into me when I was about to jump her. She was laughing as she said she should leave at least one of us alive. Even now, I can't get the sound of that voice out of my head. And as I've grown, the marks have only gotten larger. She told me she wanted me to remember what'd been done to me, and said if I joined a freak show I'd be set for the rest of my life."

Without malice or resentment, Elena's tone had the stoicism of an old woman, but her emotions burned beneath the words like a blazing fireball. That she'd been able to cling to those feelings for a dozen years without going insane was surely a fearful accomplishment.

Closing her top, Elena looked down at the ground. The emptiness that came after her explosion of emotion gnawed away at her confidence.

With the bundle of weapons over one shoulder, D walked off into the ruins without saying a word, leaving Elena there alone. But as the figure was walking away, he then said something. "Come on," was what it sounded like to Elena. Perhaps it'd been something else, but that was good enough for her. Delight coursing through every inch of her, the girl followed.

The bags D had unloaded a day earlier were still there.

"It'll be night soon," said Elena. "I'll fix something to eat. You can't very well fight those bastards on an empty stomach. So, where would your pans—," she began to ask, then hastily cupped her hand over her mouth. "You don't want any dinner, do you?"

"That's right. If you want anything to eat, you'll have to make your own arrangements."

"You don't even have any bacon or bread?"

"No," D replied.

"I guess you never figured you'd have anyone else around. Sorry— I didn't mean anything personal by that. I'll go get some food and a pan and stuff. You do at least drink coffee, don't you?"

"Weren't you supposed to be going soon?" asked the Hunter.

"I can't believe you could work as a Vampire Hunter if you're so quick to believe everything everyone tells you."

Carrying the bundle of longswords, D walked off deeper into the ruins.

"This'll be ready in no time," Elena called out to him.

"I'll be back soon," the Hunter replied.

True to his word, he returned less than ten minutes later empty-handed.

"What happened to the swords?"

"I spread them around."

"You don't say," Elena remarked as she handed him a cup of steaming brew. "You know," she continued, "I'm curious as to why you came to our village. Because I'd heard that usually even if a Vampire Hunter found a Noble, he'd just let it go unless he'd been hired."

"I've been hired."

Elena fairly bugged her eyes at his reply. "By who?!" she blurted out.

"Someone who asked me not to say."

If that was actually the case, the young man's lips would remain tight as stone. Elena quickly threw in the towel. All she knew for certain was that he was here with her now. That would have to be enough. Sooner or later, he was going to leave.

The girl swallowed her watery sorrows along with her warm beverage.

"You suppose they'll come?" she asked as she wrapped both hands around her cup.

"Yes. I don't know whether or not they'll go after the village, but they'll want to take care of me."

"But that bitch asked you to kill her knights before!"

"And do you believe everything a Noble tells you?"

"No—so stop teasing me!" Elena cried, growing bright red. Although she didn't think he was actually mocking her, she couldn't really be sure—when he never smiled and was always such a stick in the mud, it was really hard to say for certain.

"If I'm going to kill them, I have to fight them," said D. "Given their immense motivation, they'll be ready to fight to the death. What's more, they'll have been punished for their unauthorized attack on the villagers."

"I don't get that, either. How could they go against the princess? I could understand the Nobility murdering villagers, but why would the knights? Is that supposed to be their idea of loyalty?"

"Perhaps."

The Hunter's terse answer made Elena forget what she was about to say. Silence descended, and the only thing she could feel was the wind that stroked her cheek.

"Are you scared?" asked D.

"Yeah," she replied. She felt terribly meek. "But being here with you, I should be feeling pretty confident. Don't look at me. I'm shaking like a leaf. I've been on my own for a dozen years, and I was never afraid of anything in all that time. I always planned on taking out the Noble and her knights, even if it meant I got taken down in the process. Nothing anyone in the village said ever bothered me. And yet now, I'm scared. I feel like a baby could whip me. Why did you have to come to our village? And why'd you make such a coward out of me . . . ?"

"There comes a time when everyone, man or woman, young or old, has to take up arms. Even the cowards. You're out on the Frontier," D told her.

An incredible scene drifted to the fore in Elena's mind. It wasn't her parents being attacked by a pale young woman. Nor was it herself being slashed by the White Knight. It was the very embodiment of beauty getting back up after the Blue Knight's lance had pierced his abdomen.

"I was wondering—aren't you in pain?" asked the girl.

"Pain?"

"From last night. That bastard put his lance clean through you—even for a dhampir, that's gotta hurt, right?"

"Does the thought of that bother you?"

"It might," Elena replied, trying to be evasive. She suddenly felt she didn't want him to see her as weak. Even she couldn't fathom the turn her emotions were taking.

"The pain I felt when it stabbed into me was no different from what an ordinary person would feel," D replied.

Elena remained gazing intently at him, but for a few seconds she couldn't say a word. He bled. He felt pain, too. How many times over would this gorgeous man die in the course of his life? Elena shuddered—she seemed to shake with every bit of energy she had. And when the shaking subsided, her fear had gone. The intense nature of D's answer had changed the very face of the girl.

"We've got a few hours until sunset. Take a rest."

With those words, D set his cup down and stood up.

Not speaking as she watched him leave, Elena slowly counted to ten before starting off after him. Although she didn't really think she could go unnoticed or even manage to trail him very well, she simply had to satisfy her curiosity. There had to be something to these ruins. It seemed to her as if D had been aware of that from the very start and had come out here seeking it.

In the center of the ruins, D knelt before one of the stone columns and ran his fingers around its base. Elena knew that ancient letters and symbols were inscribed there. When she was just a child, the wind and rain had already worn the markings away into illegibility, but she wondered if the young man would be able to decipher the past.

"Come over here," D said, the abrupt command knocking the wind from Elena.

"You don't believe in keeping much secret, I guess," she said as she walked over to him. "What did this used to be? I mean, I can't believe how interested you are in this place. Don't tell me it holds some kind of secret about the Nobility."

"That's right," the Hunter replied.

"Tell me, then. I'll probably wind up dead tonight. I don't wanna go out wondering about this."

"These are the ruins of a fortress," D said nonchalantly.

"A fortress?! Whose?"

"I don't know. From what I could read of the remaining inscriptions, it belonged to humans. And it's rather ancient—more than two thousand years old."

"A fortress from two millennia ago—this area must've been a lot wilder back then. I wonder if colonists could've built it."

"I don't know any more than that."

A question suddenly burst free of the girl's brain. Elena made a desperate effort to recapture it, but before she could pop it like a soap bubble, it floated off her lips.

"When you came to our village, you headed straight out here. You knew about this place beforehand, didn't you?"

"Yes."

"I don't think a Vampire Hunter would come all the way out here to investigate some ruins, so I have to wonder if you weren't hired to do this, too."

"It'll be twilight soon," D said as he looked up at the heavens.

The sunlight held a tinge of blue. Two shadows fell on the stone floor. One was vivid, the other faint.

"I guess so," Elena said, facing the manor. Soon a light sparked in one of its windows. That was the call to arms. "I wonder if the princess and her three knights will all come," she mused.

In her imagination, the ecstatic Elena painted a picture of herself and D fighting side-by-side, soaked in gore.

In no time, the moon came out.

II

"The moon is up," said the Black Knight. He was in a room in the manor, and the royal blue of the night sky was visible through a spot where the ceiling had collapsed.

"Are you absolutely determined to go? The princess has given us no such mandate," said the Red Knight, who'd been standing behind his stationary compatriot and watching him for some time.

"I realize that. And that is why I've waited until night. Given the circumstances, the princess may elect to send us out. Or perhaps she'll give the order for us to accompany her. However, even if she doesn't, I'm going. You yourself saw the way the Blue Knight died. The one who killed him must be made to pay, and those of us who yet live must exact that payment."

"Even if that means disregarding the will of the princess?"

"Aye," the Black Knight replied without a second's hesitation.

Gazing at him with adoration, the Red Knight said, "I shall go with you."

Now it was the Black Knight's turn to ask the same question. "Even if it means disobeying the princess?"

"Yes."

"You'll meet the same fate that I have."

"I don't care," said the Red Knight. Only now, his voice echoed with a certain something that was neither purely rage nor pity. The punishment that'd been carried out in the stained-glass chamber had been branded into his retinas. And the ghastly results of it were before his very eyes.

The Black Knight's right arm had been taken off at the shoulder.

"Then you're to follow my directions," the Black Knight insisted as he turned to the Red Knight.

"I swear it."

"Obey the princess's instructions. I forbid you to disobey her. If you ever so much as harbor such thoughts again, you'll be marked a traitor."

For a moment the Red Knight was stunned, but a second later he began to say, "But I—"

"No arguments," the Black Knight stated firmly. The steely gravity of his tone repressed the rebellious fervor in the Red Knight. "The princess's tack now is different from that in the past. Perhaps the weariness I feel comes from her. However, I am no Noble. I can't imagine what kind of thoughts might instill such feelings in her, or how those emotions might manifest. Most likely—"

Something hidden in the unfinished portion of that last sentence made the Red Knight grow tense.

"—it will bode ill for all involved? How right you are!"

At the sound of that echoing voice, the two knights looked all around in astonishment, and then turned back the way they'd been facing.

Beside a stone pillar on the point of collapse stood the princess. To her rear, the darkness was crushed beneath a spreading mass of roses, roses, and more roses. And their glow.

"Aren't you the stubborn one," the princess remarked, skewering the Black Knight with her smile.

The two fell to one knee.

"However," the Noblewoman continued, "you won't be going anywhere tonight. You're to remain here."

"If I might explain, Princess."

"You needn't bother," the woman said with a sweep of the white rose in her hand. Leaving a trail of light behind it, the glowing bloom was swallowed by the darkness. "I understand how angry all of you must be. But that Hunter is a formidable opponent. Do you want to end up like the Blue Knight?"

"That shall depend on the Hunter," the Black Knight replied with all due respect and fealty.

"No. I shall be the one to go see him."

The two knights looked up at their mistress, and for the first time since entering her service they dared to voice their opposition, shouting, "You mustn't!"

Although the Red Knight was shaken as the Black Knight glared at him, the princess didn't seem at all perturbed by their outburst.

"Never fear. I shall have a different escort," she said.

"The White Knight?"

"No. A group you've not seen these last two centuries."

The Black Knight alone seemed to understand, as he looked up at her and said, "You don't mean—*them*?"

"None other."

"Princess, I say this fully prepared to accept any additional punishments. But that is one thing you simply cannot do!"

"Why is that?!" she inquired.

"As soon as you let them loose outside, it'll be a scene of bloody carnage," the Black Knight replied. "I'm quite certain they could slay a dhampir. They could annihilate the villagers as well. However, the bloodthirsty beasts will forget your commands and leave your domain, completely indiscriminate in their unending search for blood. That cannot be. That is not what our wise princess would do. Oh, Princess—whatever has come over you?"

"Over *me*?"

"Once again, I ask this prepared to suffer a thousand deaths," the Black Knight said, sounding as if he were coughing out blood instead of words.

Listening intently, the Red Knight hung his head without saying a word.

"Princess, you have changed over the last few years. Though I can't describe exactly how, you seem like a different person. I cannot comprehend your thoughts or feelings, milady."

"My, how you pry into my affairs," the enchanting princess spat. "Red Knight, do you share his opinion?"

"I do, milady," he replied, but the very second he spoke, a flash of black shot from beside him and knocked him to the floor before he could avoid it.

"How dare you say such a thing—Please overlook his insolence, milady," the Black Knight apologized with a deep bow.

"Good enough," said the princess. "But I said I would send them, and send them I shall. As for you, Black Knight—you're to be incarcerated. Red Knight, lock him away."

Either the Red Knight remained conscious when knocked to the floor or he'd since regained his senses, because he gazed at the Black Knight and responded with a troubled, "Yes, milady."

Still holding a rose in her mouth, the princess said, "Do you intend to interfere with me, even if it means you must go through the Red Knight? Or will you turn your sword against me?"

"No. Your orders will be followed," the Black Knight replied. His answer had a bitter taste to it.

The darkness grew denser and denser while the four-colored roses glowed stunningly.

Poised with his left hand resting against the pillar, D turned suddenly in the direction of the manor. There wasn't a sound on the night wind. Nevertheless, the hand he had pressed against the pillar asked him, "Did you hear that?"

"They're coming," D replied succinctly.

"That they are. Ten of them, I'd say. On horseback. But what I sense isn't the knights. With those guys, you can't tell if they're dead or alive. But these characters are all definitely dead."

"Wraith knights," D muttered.

"Bingo. And they've got this awfully powerful energy protecting them. That'd have to be the woman's doing."

"Are they coming?"

D turned to the entrance of the ruin and replied to the girl who sat there with an electron lantern in hand. "They'll be here soon."

Elena got right up, without nervousness, hesitation or even fear.

"This is what I've been waiting for," said the girl. "Where did you figure we'd fight them?"

"You're going to be here."

"What do you mean?!" Elena cried.

"It's not the knights that are on the way, but a band of dead men. And those who've died once can't be killed a second time."

"Well, what are you gonna do then?"

"I have no choice but to kill them."

Although Elena found that to be the very epitome of contradiction, on reconsideration she decided this young man's skill with a blade probably would be enough to kill the dead once more.

"At this point, I'm not about to sit back and be a good little girl. Take me with you," the biker told D. "Hell, if you insist on turning me down, I'll just go off and fight anyway."

"Staying in the ruins is part of the battle, too."

"That's just double-talk," Elena said as she searched in the bike for another weighted chain.

"We'll see soon enough. But when the time comes, I need you to be right in here."

"Really?"

"Really," D replied.

"I believe you. And I won't have you worrying about me at a time like this."

Not saying a word, D left her and set off across the plains that lay between them and the castle.

There was a breeze. The green grass swayed in the moonlight. And there stood the Hunter—that alone formed a picture. Any artist who could've committed to canvas the inner thoughts of the young man as he stood there between life and death would've become a prisoner of his own madness, although the resulting painting would surely endure forever as a treasure of the art world.

"Here they come," a hoarse voice said some five minutes after the Hunter had taken that position on the plain. The ruins were roughly five hundred yards away.

The riders approaching across the grasslands seemed to float in a horrifying sort of slow motion. Both mounts and riders were covered by dull gray armor. Reaching a spot about thirty feet shy of D, they halted. Their movements were so quiet that all but the most intent of listeners would've missed the sounds completely.

"The wraith knights—I've heard of them," said the Hunter's left hand.

There was no reply at all, as if it had been addressing the moon.

The ash gray figures lingered there in the moonlight like veritable ghosts. *Shreee!* squealed the leader's blade as it slid from the scabbard on the knight's hip. At the same time, the other nine drew their weapons in unison. Three had swords, three more bows, and the last three had lances. Their weapons differed little from those of the four knights.

"Where are the princess and the others?" asked D.

One of riders raised its head and laughed. But no voice came out. Its laughter had stopped.

D was up over its head. The Hunter's thirty-foot leap had no doubt been faster than the wraith knight's eyes could follow. With a grating sound and a shower of sparks the blade of D's sword crumpled, but it also plowed right through the knight from the top of its head all the way down to its abdomen.

As he came back to earth, D looked at his foe. The feeling he'd gotten from his blade hadn't been ordinary resistance.

Something like a white fog poured from the crack in the iron. In places, the cloud glittered as if it were laced with silver. Once the fog had fallen from the horse back to the ground, it took on a human form. An insect on the plain came into contact with the fog-like being and suddenly fell over.

"Death essence?" said the Hunter's left hand.

Some might've called it a supernatural aura or an eerie miasma. But as it took the life of anything that touched it right on the spot, "death essence" seemed the most fitting name. This was the true form of the band of ghostly riders.

The hazy mass moved toward D, seeming to be both borne on the wind and fighting it at the same time.

The Hunter no longer had a sword. And even if he'd still possessed one, it would've been impossible to cut this amorphous and unearthly cloud.

As for D—he did nothing but stand still.

Elena had no knowledge of D's deadly battle. The darkness had already grown quite heavy, and her eyes couldn't see more than a hundred fifty feet. An unsettling mist seemed to billow up around her, covering her skin with goose bumps. Giving a shudder, Elena held out her electron lantern.

Something suddenly dampened the light. A single white rose had landed on the top of the lantern. And Elena discovered that its thin stem had sunk right through the metal roof of her light.

"But this is—," she began to say, and then her lantern went out.

There in the darkness, with nothing save the moonlight, the rose alone glowed as if it were ablaze.

"A gift to replace that boorish light of yours."

Raising her gaze from the rose that'd kept her riveted, Elena found the lovely princess standing before her. Aside from D, she had to wonder who else would've looked so perfect standing out in the moonlight. Elena got the feeling she could see the scenery behind the woman right through the surpassing paleness of her countenance.

"What are you supposed to be, the vanguard or something?" the biker asked. She felt strangely calm.

"I suppose I may be, at that. My interest was piqued when I learned you were out here. No doubt that was all D's doing. There's no way a lowly human could understand the significance of this place, even though it was humans that constructed it."

"Two thousand years ago, right?"

Donning a somewhat surprised expression, the princess said, "Information courtesy of D, I presume. He's also bound to notice me here sooner or later."

"If I finish you off before that, it won't matter either way," Elena said as the weighted end of a chain spilled from her right hand. This one was a lot thicker than what she usually carried.

Still staring fixedly at the princess, Elena began to spin the chain in a circle with her right hand. The growling *whup whup whup* of it became a whistling *shooshooshoo*, and then it moved beyond the realm of sound.

"My, aren't you the skillful one," the princess declared, clapping her hands.

Though Elena realized the woman was needling her, she couldn't afford to get angry. Her consciousness was focused solely on destroying the lovely princess.

Without making a sound, the princess moved behind a stone pillar to avoid the shrilly whistling weight at the end of the chain. But the chain went right after her.

"Dear me!" the woman cried in surprise, her exclamation mingled with the sound of steel biting into stone.

While it was unclear what kind of trick the girl had used, the chain that pursued the princess had wrapped around both the Noblewoman and the pillar with enough force to dig into both flesh and stone.

"You fell for it, sucker!" Elena roared with delight as she raced over to the princess.

There wasn't a shred of mercy in the girl. In her right hand she held a finely honed stake of unfinished wood. Raising it high over her head, she shouted, "Here's your ticket to the afterlife, your majesty!"

But as Elena brought the weapon down, four shades of light shimmered before her eyes.

"Oh!" the girl cried when the hand she waved through the glowing blobs told her they were no illusion. They had substance.

There were red roses. And blue. And even black.

Though Elena batted them away time and again, more and more new flowers surrounded her, obscuring her view and, worse yet, forming a dazzling riot of color that assailed her brain and left her dizzy.

"Damn it all!" the biker growled.

From the madly eddying flowers a length of chain looped out and wound around a lintel that connected two of the stone columns. As Elena swung up on it, the four-tone stream flowed after her.

Up on the lintel, Elena pulled a tiny oilpaper packet from her shirt pocket and shook the white powder it contained over her own head. And it was a sight to see as every flower that touched her then curled its petals and lost its color before falling back to earth.

"Mama Kipsch's special herbicide! Have some!" Elena shouted, and she was about to scatter the rest of the powder over the princess down below when the breath was knocked out of her.

The other chain was tangled on the ground, and there was no sign of the pale figure.

"Here I am! Over here!"

As she whipped around to face the voice she heard behind her, Elena let fly with the chain she still had.

Winding it around her right hand, the princess smiled elegantly. "It would be so easy to kill you," she said to the girl. "Like so."

With one tug of her hand she easily snatched away Elena's chain.

"Would you like me to strangle you with this? Or would you prefer that I tear your limbs off one by one?"

Beads of sweat formed at a furious rate on Elena's brow.

III

The wind began to sweep across the plain—a wind that carried death. Borne on it, the death essence might drift anywhere. And any living thing it touched would perish.

At present, it was squaring off against D. The white humanoid shape spread into an amorphous cloud, then gusted at the Hunter. As D leapt backward, he raised his left hand as if to ward off his attacker, and the fog enveloped it. The hand turned a dull brown color, but quickly returned to its original hue.

"That's one hell of a death essence, all right," a pained voice said. It was still coughing. "There's no way to kill this thing from the outside. I might be able to handle one or two, but if I were to suck up any more than that, I could be a goner. Wait a sec and I'll look into a few things."

At that point, one of the other riders tumbled noisily from the saddle. A white substance seeped from the armor and circled around behind D's back.

Several streaks of light flew from D's left hand at a terrific speed, yet after piercing the man-shaped cloud of fog, they wobbled lazily for another three feet before falling to the ground. Now stained black, the bare wooden needles crumbled, rotten to the very core.

By the look of things, any weapon—be it a sword or even a bullet—would be utterly useless here.

The fog laughed. No, it might've just been the fault of the wind shaking its upper body a tad, but the night air had definitely carried a sound that was not a sound, and it had resembled laughter.

The fog slowly drifted closer to D from the front. Behind him was the other mass. A split second before the latter could wrap its pale arms about D's body, the Hunter rose into the air. As part of the death essence closing on him continued to flow forward, the rest of the mass spun around with terrific force, while the cloud of death essence to D's rear backed away with equal decisiveness.

As D landed, he twisted his body. The blow he'd narrowly escaped split the tail of his coat as the lance jabbed into the earth. In rapid succession a second and a third followed—and though the attacks came at a speed no average person or even professional warrior could've dodged, D narrowly slipped through them without incident and dove into the very ranks of the wraith knights.

Two swords flew up with a metallic rasp, and a pair of the wraiths were unhorsed. It's doubtful even the wraith knights could believe that the lance D held in his hand was the same one that'd just been aimed at him. However, even D would find it impossible to destroy a shapeless cloud unaffected by any weapon. How would he fight it? And how could he kill it?

Elena quickly wiped the sweat from her brow with her left hand. If it were to run into her eyes, it would be the death of her. The princess was ten feet ahead. And she'd taken away one of the biker's chains. She glared at the princess for all she was worth. If she let the Noblewoman break her spirit, she'd be beat.

The princess looked back at Elena.

"I remember you," the princess said with a knowing nod. "Your parents and siblings all ended up on my dinner menu. And I believe the White Knight gave you a wound you'd carry for the rest of your life. How interesting."

Her grinning face was as bewitching as the moon, yet as innocent as that of the purest maiden. And that was why Elena was as chilled as if she'd been doused with ice water.

"Now that I think of it, crushing you alone would accomplish nothing. Perhaps I should find another use for you. Oh, I know," she laughed. "I shall give you a different wound."

As the smile on the princess's lips grew broader and more unsettling, Elena turned away out of reflex. The more beautiful a Noble's smile was, the stronger the human urge was to look away. And because of that, the girl didn't notice the white rose flying from the princess's right hand. When it stuck in her left breast, she felt a slight pain and looked down. But the rose was already gone.

"What did you do?"

"See for yourself. Look at your chest."

Like a woman possessed, Elena tore open the front of her shirt. The revolting "x" was fading. But in return, something smaller but even more terrifying had been etched on her left breast—a tattoo of a white rose so exquisitely detailed it seemed it could only be the handiwork of an angel.

Despair sucked the strength from her very cells. For in Elena's eyes, nothing could've been crueler than being marked with this symbol of the Nobility. Staggering, she fell from the rock lintel. The princess's hand caught her by the scruff of the neck.

But even as she was hauled back up, Elena couldn't so much as manage to ask the princess to kill her. Her face was like that of a corpse, and a cheery voice whispered in her ear, "No need to be so despondent. Soon you'll feel ever so much better. Once you've experienced the privileges of one of my servants with your own flesh, that is."

And as she finished speaking, the princess suddenly looked down below her. A slight tremor had reached her through the ground.

"An earthquake?" she muttered as a shadow spread across her beautiful countenance. "Does this hateful fortress yet live? Impossible!"

Her body swayed as the quaking of the earth and its related rumblings overwhelmed the night.

"Oh, my—this is quite a pickle," the princess said, although where she'd learned such an expression was anyone's guess.

Putting Elena under one arm, the princess leapt down to the ground. From above her, tiny fragments of stone rained down.

"I don't have the time to wait around and see what happens next. I'm also curious to see how D and his playmates made out."

The woman then started off across the plain. Elena never left her grip for a second.

Knights were closing on the Hunter from either side. The one on his right had a lance, while the one on his left had a longsword. Just as they were about to bring their weapons down on D, the knights swapped armaments—the one on the right took the sword and the one on the left the lance.

When the weapons in play changed, an opponent had to alter his strategy accordingly. And if the exchange could be done in a matter of seconds, it could only result in confusion on the part of the person preparing to defend himself. In the case of simultaneous attacks, there would really be no way at all to defend oneself.

The lance and sword swung home.

Surprise was not an emotion the wraiths possessed. Nevertheless, the vibrations that swept through the air in that instant were nothing but pure shock. The sword blade slashing down from the right was caught by D's left hand, while a lance in the Hunter's other hand parried the lance that came at him from the left. That would've been strange enough if the Hunter had been facing them. But just before the wraith knights launched their attack—in the very instant they traded weapons—they saw D turn his back to them. Though they realized he'd seen through their plan of attack, they'd been unsure of what to do next. They'd already struck at him with the lance and sword.

Once he'd snatched away the longsword, D made a bound. But who in the world could leap onto the back of a horse as it was galloping by?

D could, and he did. Standing on back of the steed carrying the sword-wielding knight, he kicked the rider off the mount and seized the reins. Seeing this, the other knights charged him en masse.

"D, give me some of your blood," his left hand said. "It's only a temporary measure, but I've come up with a substance these boys aren't gonna like. Hurry!"

Taking his hand off the reins and holding his longsword with his teeth, D put his right wrist against the blade and gave a hard pull. The warm liquid that spilled out landed in the palm of his left hand. And his palm opened its mouth and gulped down the fresh blood.

"Stick out your sword!"

Taking the sword he clenched between his teeth in his right hand, D ran his left hand along the blade. When vermilion smoke billowed from his palm to discolor the blade, the riders ahead of him launched a number of arrows at him. They weren't wooden— even the shafts and fletchings were iron. If they were to strike a human body, the impact would rip the flesh apart.

D stopped every last one of them with his left hand. It looked more like he was catching paper airplanes. As the Hunter rode right by the knight, who'd been paralyzed and without a chance to nock another arrow, his longsword flashed out. The wraith's torso ripped open.

Without even looking back, D raced toward his next opponent— a white fog was closing on him from the fore. Apparently, it'd realized it would only be at a disadvantage fighting him in its armor. Pulling on the reins to circle around to the right, D swung his blade.

The fog shuddered. The part that approximated a human head split in two, and then began to fuse together once more. But the pieces didn't stay together. As it moved its hand-like portions, the figure lost the details of its shape and became a mass of fog that dropped to the ground. Two or three spasms shook the mass, and then it barely managed to rise again. Staggering all the while, it started back across the plain to the manor. The rider that followed after it must've been the same one that'd been slashed through the torso seconds earlier.

The Hunter's foes were unnerved and restless. From the very start, they'd known he wasn't the kind to meet them with conventional tactics. They all backed away at once.

The survivors then launched arrows—not at D, but toward the sky. Apparently the missiles had some sort of special mechanism, because in mid-flight the tail ends of them began to leave glowing trails before they were enveloped in dazzling flames about thirty feet above the earth. What's more, they neither rose nor dropped, hanging in the sky dribbling sparks—and then a second later, they exploded. A halo bright enough to burn a sharp shadow of D on the ground spread out, and from the center of it a number of fiery streaks raced out at D and the plains. Flames billowed up. Night became day, and the flames spreading across the ground quickly melted together and leapt to new locations like wildfire.

Avoiding the flames, D retreated to the entrance to the ruins.

More fire arrows went up, giving rise to additional walls of flame. The wind grew fiercer. The plains were burning. And as the flames spread as far as the eye could see, they somehow looked like water. Like a glittering sea stretching out to the night horizon.

From their steeds, the wraith knights nocked more fiery arrows. Twice as long and twice as thick, they were set to spread the blaze not only to the ruins but into the very village of Sacri itself.

It was at just that moment that the earth rumbled. One after another the horses threw their riders, and then the mounts themselves fell over. The shaking was more than that of a simple earthquake. Unseen waves surged through the air, and the knights caught up in the turbulence were knocked flat in the blink of an eye. White masses wriggled out through gaps in the gray armor, but as a second wave washed over them they went into spasms, and then moved no more. And the waves were equally ruthless as they assailed the wraith knights that'd already taken flight.

"That will be quite enough."

D turned in the direction of the voice and found the princess and Elena.

"And here I believed all this time that I was the only one who knew the secret of these ruins. You don't miss a trick, do you?" the lovely princess said with a shrug after looking at what had seemed to be nothing save humble remains.

The fortification had been constructed centuries earlier by a human sect with wisdom that put them on par with the Nobility, yet it still retained its ancient capabilities. Naturally, the only reason those forces had gone into action just now was D's own supernatural powers.

"Hand over the girl," said D.

"This girl," the princess replied, "is already one of my kind. Though to be honest, I just finished doing the honors. Are you going to try and save her, D? It won't be as easy with her as it was with the others. I've dealt her a harsh blow, you see."

Elena's expression was vacant. Tears wouldn't even flow from her eyes.

"I'll give you the girl. You needn't do anything about her, D. Your job is to kill me, is it not? This waif is no part of that. Just leave her to grow paler night after night till her fangs pop out and she runs amok, drinking blood indiscriminately. Even if you do nothing, I'm sure the villagers will be good enough to dispose of her. You did well to send my wraith knights into retreat, but apparently you weren't up to the task of destroying them. Oh, my lovely visitor," she laughed, "today's festivities are but a dress rehearsal. The main event will come tomorrow or the next day, or perhaps a year from now."

"Didn't you want me to get rid of your knights?" D asked in a tone like ice.

As if it'd just dawned on her, the enchanting princess responded, "Oh, that's right! I did, didn't I? Then I'll bring them out tomorrow. Three against one would simply be too dangerous, so we'll take them one by one. I'll start sending them tomorrow night. You'll just have to wait and see which one I choose to send first."

And with a haughty laugh, the princess turned the rose she held in her hand upside down. Tiny flecks that glowed in the moonlight rained down on the earth.

"Very well, that shall be all for this evening," she said. "Oh, I'll thank you not to run after me with that ratty old sword. Well, as they said in one of the ancient tongues, '*Zaijian!*'"

As the princess headed for her manor, D galloped after her. Although her horse practically flew, his mount was swifter. But he'd only chased her for a few yards when the ground suddenly swelled up before him. The soil had taken on four hues. It was a wall made of roses. High and wide it stretched, like a barricade to check D's advance.

"That's my rose rampart. Can you get by it?" the princess sneered in the distance, and D halted before a wall of flowers easily thirty feet high and half a mile long, even the very presence of the Noblewoman faded away.

"There's just no figuring that woman," his left hand said. "She's seriously out to kill you, yet she also meant it when she asked you to take out her knights. I don't have a clue what she's really thinking. Anyway, what are you gonna do about the girl? You just gonna forget about her?"

The Fallen Ones

CHAPTER 7

I

D carried Elena's limp form to Mama Kipsch's place. The crone who'd come out rubbing sleepily at her eyes had performed an examination on the girl and immediately discovered the rose on her chest.

"This is much more serious than those flowers the other night. Based on what I've just seen, it looks like it goes all the way down to the bone."

"Can you cure her?" asked the Hunter.

Looking at D with visible surprise, the old woman said, "Are you worried about her? I'd gotten the impression that the life or death of anyone else was a world away from you. You mean to tell me our cries actually reach your ears?"

"I just asked if you can cure her."

Shrugging her shoulders, Mama Kipsch replied, "You should know a lot more about that than me. As things stand, there's not a thing that can be done for her."

"Well, I leave her to you," D said, and then he turned and headed for the door.

"Hold on there! You're the only one who can make her better."

"I thought you said nothing could be done," D remarked.

"I was talking about the way things are right now. With the right trappings, I should be able to do something."

Although the woman truly expected some sort of response, she grimaced on receiving none and said, "On the western edge of this domain there's a village called Zamba. In the Temple of the Inner Body, there blooms a single prismatic rose right about *here*—in what would be someone's gut. And it's been there for the last two thousand years. Bring it back here. The village and temple haven't known human habitation for a good three centuries—the only things to get in your way would be monsters and evil sprites and the beasts of the plains. And that stuff should be minor league to you."

"My job is to destroy the lady of the manor," D stated flatly.

"Heck, I know that. At my age, I wouldn't ask anyone to step into the jaws of death just out of the goodness of their heart. I'll offer compensation. The princess has put that tattoo pretty deep on the girl. In trying to get the same result as biting her without doing it the old-fashioned way, she's drained a lot of the life from her victim. Seeing how sharp the tattoo is should be proof enough of that. I could try to get rid of it, but the girl would just wind up an invalid. Of course, she'd be a Noble invalid, but even I've never seen anything like that before."

Here the witch doctor gave a big belly laugh, but when D didn't so much as crack a smile, she awkwardly continued, "At any rate, it doesn't matter how good of a Hunter you are; getting rid of an invalid Noble must be a heck of a lot easier than taking out a healthy one. Here's your compensation. What do you say?"

"You've got a deal," D replied easily.

With a wry smile, Mama Kipsch said, "You know, you've got a very, very unfortunate character. At this rate, you'll go through your whole life being chalked up as a cold-hearted brute. Granted, I'm sure you probably don't give a rat's behind about that. Count on no one but yourself—of all the folks I've ever met, only you and two others could honestly say they live that way. And I don't think I'm likely to see another anytime soon."

And then she stood up and placed her hand on D's shoulder. For some reason, he made no attempt to avoid it.

"I know you think you're doing this as a cut-and-dried business deal, but that's just not the feeling I get. I was banking on that when I asked you. Do what you can for us."

The crone suddenly realized she couldn't feel anything under her fingertips. The youth of heavenly beauty had disappeared through the door—out into the darkness that suited him far better.

"D . . ."

The muttered name made Mama Kipsch turn.

Elena stood in the doorway of the examination room. One look at her eyes was enough to show that her consciousness was fragmented. In her present state, the only thing that could've carried her this far was the man whose name had just spilled from her bloodless lips.

"Please . . . don't . . . leave me . . . ," Elena mumbled as tears began to roll from her eyes.

It was dawn by the time D arrived in the village of Zamba. The kind of pony express that handled ordinary mail deliveries would've taken an estimated eight hours to make that run, but he'd done it in less than five. During the trip, a number of people had seen D and hidden themselves by the side of the road. Galloping along with a cloud of dust in his wake, the Hunter in black must've been a terrifying sight for the average traveler.

As Mama Kipsch had said, it was a desolate region of mountains and rivers, without a single timber remaining to mark where the village had been. But the Temple of the Inner Body still survived in the hilly region on the western extreme of the village, a building constructed with a technique that allowed stone and iron to be blended together. And yet, the parts with high stone content had been eroded by wind and rain, leaving great holes gaping sinisterly in the structure.

As its name suggested, the temple was the sixty-foot-high and hundred-foot-long image of a giant deity in repose carved untold ages ago from the heart of one of the hills—literally formed from the core of the hill, with an entrance in the head that allowed visitors to go inside. But in this case, "inner body" also had a second meaning. Similar structures dotted the Frontier—in the southwestern sectors they were particularly prevalent—but the fact was that none of them were very well-preserved, and almost all had become the dens of supernatural beasts or the lairs of criminals.

Leaving his overworked cyborg horse outside with its cooling systems on, D entered the body/temple of the gargantuan god with nothing save the sword on his back. His weapon was one of the blades he'd hidden around the ruins on the outskirts of Sacri. As he was leaving the village, he'd swung by the blacksmith's place, and a woman who must've been his wife appeared to tell the Hunter her husband had gone off to a special site known to him alone to put a soul into the sword he'd been charged with making. He'd left the night before, she said, and still hadn't returned.

A strange sight greeted D.

If an artist or sculptor of exceptional talent were to visit this place, the supreme heresy inherent in its design and the wealth of horrifying imagery—not the stuff of nightmare, but bald-faced reality—couldn't help but drive them to lunacy. A human being couldn't conceive of what the inside of a god looked like. If they wanted to find out, they had no choice but to come here.

Opening the door in the top of its head and stepping inside what must've been the brain of the deity, the Hunter found row upon row of pleats in a barely translucent wax-like alloy. The creases housed statues of this god or other deities with a rich patina, as well as talismans carved with unsettling pictographs. The passageway suddenly narrowed into what was apparently the esophagus, and once a visitor had passed from there into the torso, the human sense of direction could no longer be trusted.

Was this actually how the internal organs of a god were laid out?

The terribly flat floor suddenly became a series of wild grooves. At one point D was actually walking across the ceiling, and the passageways that'd clearly existed vanished when he took his eye off them for a second. Nothing here had been constructed in a straight line, and yet the curves didn't really feel like they curved either. While he was certain he'd been advancing in a straight line, he also got the feeling he was going around in circles. The very fact that he could feel like he was going in a straight line and running in circles at the same time was truly bizarre.

Neither the human body nor its mind were meant to deal with this. As proof, the skeletons scattered at D's feet had rusty red knives and swords poking from their chests—either wounds they'd inflicted on themselves or each other. The remaining human and monster bones were most likely left by creatures who'd wandered into this maze that defied Euclidean geometry and had fallen to exhaustion and starvation.

D advanced down that inhuman, maddening path without the slightest delay.

What manner of being had carved all this? As if to praise the greatness of their faith, the ceiling, walls, and floor were all engraved with secret incantations or covered with colorful murals.

Finally, D halted in a certain vast section. Apparently light from the outside world was somehow channeled into this chamber, as there was sufficient illumination. What D saw was a gaudily hued dais of a lumpy, misshapen material like cooled lava with a metallic altar set on top. The altar in turn was crowned by a clear, prism-shaped container enclosing a single rose that evinced the loveliest hues.

Reaching out for the bloom with his hand, D then stopped as if he'd had some portent. The mistress of a rose garden that bloomed in splendor on moonlit nights, and the prismatic rose that could be considered the symbol of the very deity around it—it didn't seem likely these two could both exist in the same remote area and not be related. There had to be a common thread connecting them somewhere.

"There's an awfully primitive trap built into the altar. It has the odor of machine oil," said a hoarse voice.

"I'm aware of that," D replied, once again reaching out for the container and touching it. Before he'd even raised the bloom, a switch must've been triggered, and there was the whine of a motor that then quickly died out.

"Looks like it'd be best to get out of here fast!"

Not appearing to have any objection to the hoarse voice's suggestion, D started back the way he'd come without so much as a backward glance.

The walls warped abruptly, taking new forms, making different ridges and crevices, forming other passageways. Apparently the rule was that no intruder was to leave again.

"Oh, my! I guess the spirit of whatever built this thing still remains here," the Hunter's left hand groaned. "It'd be a discredit to the god to let its symbol be taken. Looks like getting out will be tough."

D turned around.

The area around the altar remained unchanged, utterly fixed. Approaching the platform, D casually drew his sword. The blade he was about to sink into something was then crossed by a band of light that raced toward the altar. Split in two, the altar thudded to the floor.

Turning to the wall where the light had originated, D said, "Black Knight."

It wasn't a question. He could tell from the flash who'd cut through the altar. Still, there was no sign of his foe.

"A strange place this is, and this is one of its amusements," the Black Knight said, his voice holding no surprise at the fact that his identity had been deduced. He'd understood from the very start that D was capable of as much. "Two foes, each trying to cut an opponent he can't see—although in the case of you and I, we can see even if we can't *see*. Shall we continue?"

"Very well," D responded.

That was rare. This young man was more likely to meet such an offer from his opponent with a blow from his sword rather than a single word.

Not budging a step, D stabbed into a point on the wall. His sword moved with blinding speed. There was a sharp *ching!* of steel that seemed to bite right into the marrow of the listener's spine—D had just parried another flash of light coming from a different position. But it wasn't even clear when he'd had time to pull his sword out of the wall.

D ran along the wall—this was the path that led to the gigantic figure's abdomen. It showed no further signs of changing.

Flashes of light raced from the wall in two places. The two streaks shot up, and D halted. His left arm came down, a stream of red spilling from his sleeve across the back of his hand. That was courtesy of the two streaks of light.

The air froze. It was taking on the very same nature as D's body— every molecule could tell that the gorgeous Hunter had his concentration focused on his foe. If someone were to touch him just then, the merest contact would've literally cut them, and blood would've gushed from their flesh.

Despite being on the other side of the wall, the Black Knight had said that they could see each other. That being the case, was D trying to see something new? Or would he attempt instead to see things differently?

The Hunter's right hand limned an arc. The second that same line was traced across the wall, D's body dropped off to the left side.

A hole had opened in the ground. The floor had not rotted out—rather, this was one last act of resistance against the one who'd defiled this holy place.

With his mind brutally focused on other matters, even D couldn't react instantaneously. A wide swath of light came from beyond the wall to slash deeply into his reeling form. Into the nape of his neck.

As vermilion stained the world around him, D plunged feet-first into the darkness.

II

It was pointless to wonder whether there could really be a never-ending hole within this gigantic effigy of a recumbent deity. The pit the Hunter had fallen into actually seemed to be bottomless. At least, there was no bottom that D's eyes could detect.

"You're okay, aren't you?" a voice inquired in a tone that could've been taken as either lackadaisical or hurried—though it was probably the latter.

"I'm going up," D replied.

Here were the recuperative powers of a dhampir in all their glory. Though his neck had been cut halfway through, the wound had already closed, and all that remained was a whitish line. He'd thrust the sword in his right hand into the wall to end his fall—and while that may have sounded all well and good, the fact of the matter was he was in an extremely delicate, horrific predicament. Less than four inches of his blade had gone into the wall, and the longsword was gradually levering lower and lower under D's weight. If he were to fall again, it wouldn't be a question of whether or not the Hunter would be up to another attempt, but rather whether his sword could endure it.

What's more, true to the anxiety in the voice from his left hand, D himself looked to be in incredibly rough shape, despite the fact that his tone was as cool as ever. Though the wound had closed, the blow the Black Knight had dealt him had left damage that wouldn't easily be repaired. Ordinarily, D would've kept one hand pressed to his ravaged neck while he used the other to climb up the wall.

A pale blue fire sparked in the Hunter's left hand—flames of energy spilling from the mouth of the countenanced carbuncle that'd formed on the back of it.

"Looks like even this won't work," the face groaned in apparent amazement. Grimacing, it added, "It seems he gave you one hell of a cut. I'd say that knight's not your average customer at all. Can you climb up?"

But even as the face on his hand questioned him, it felt D's body beginning to rise.

Trusting all his weight to his right hand, which held the blade he'd driven into the wall, D pushed off the sword to lift himself up. His left hand reached out and caught hold of a slight projection on the wall. Pulling the sword out, he swung upward with his left arm and jammed the blade into the wall again.

From a human perspective, it was something only a superman could've done. Working without a break, he climbed more than three hundred feet in no time, and suddenly there was a circle of light above his head.

A shadow fell across D's face. His countenance free of emotion, D looked up at the Black Knight, who stood at the brink of the pit.

The knight extended one hand, saying, "Although I don't suppose you need it, I thought I'd offer it as a courtesy nonetheless. Even if you choose to take it, you shall owe me nothing."

"What were you waiting for?" D asked softly.

The only thing supporting him was the blade of his sword. Under the circumstances, it didn't seem possible that even D would be able to respond to a stroke from the Black Knight.

"To fight," the Black Knight replied with refreshing simplicity.

"In that case—," D said, sailing through the air an instant later.

The Black Knight moved further into the corridor, and D landed in the knight's former position.

"I've returned your favor."

The gigantic black tree of a knight nodded at D's words–he had genuinely intended to pull D up out of the hole. As for D, his blade had been invested with an unvarnished will to kill as he leapt from the pit. If he'd brought it down then, the Black Knight would've been powerless to keep it from slashing him in two. What's more, the knight hadn't even known what D's intent was.

D's choice not to cut the Black Knight down when he had the chance was in repayment for the hand the knight had offered him in aid. However, to the handsome Hunter who'd come through fields of slaughter and storms of blood, this was essentially a business transaction—he did it the same way he'd fulfill the conditions of any contract.

"It's a bit cramped in here. Perhaps it would be best if we settled this outside?" the Black Knight suggested.

D saw that his opponent's voice and form were now shrouded in the unearthly aura of someone else entirely, for the knight was cursing himself for underestimating his foe.

"There's an exit not far from here. Follow me," the Black Knight said, and then he turned sharply. Was it because he figured D wouldn't come at him until they were outside? Did he still trust D, or was there another reason?

The exit the pair appeared from was in the long, muscular swell of the deity's thigh. There was a plaza in front of the temple for worship. The two of them squared off against each other in that relic of the past where now only green turf remained. Fifteen feet lay between them— one of the combatants would have to step forward at this distance.

The Black Knight remained with his weapon undrawn, and D held his blade out straight at eye level. The tip of his sword was pointed ever so slightly down. And it didn't move. The perfectly natural pose of the Black Knight wouldn't allow it to do so.

On the other hand, the Black Knight found his soul awash in admiration. For while D's stance was a common enough posture, the Hunter himself had vanished—leaving the white glint of his sword tip alone to occupy the knight's field of view. The instant D fell into the pit, the knight was certain he'd felt his blade make contact. For an ordinary person it would've been a critical wound, and even for a dhampir it'd take roughly six months to recover from such an injury. There was no way the Hunter was in top physical shape. And yet he was still so—

As if in synchronization with his own overawed thoughts, the knight's field of view suddenly expanded. D had lowered his sword.

The Black Knight stepped forward. Part of his mind screamed, *You shouldn't have done that*, and a shudder ran through him. But even as he warned himself it was an open invitation, his right hand reached around to his back with ungodly speed.

In point of fact, the Black Knight didn't know exactly what the weapon on his back was. The next thing the warrior knew, it would be there in his hands, and he'd know how to use it and what to expect from it. Of course, to get to the point where he was now, he'd undergone hellish training that'd not only left him spitting blood, but had made the very flame of life gutter within him more than once. Nevertheless, he didn't understand the principles on which his weapon operated. There was only one thing he did know—it was going to slay the Vampire Hunter right now.

A split second before he sent the blade of light flying from his weapon, the Black Knight saw that D had his arms impossibly extended above his head—in the high position. But his flash got off first in a horizontal swipe at the Hunter.

Splitting the band of light in two, D's sword continued on to sink into the Black Knight's helm. There was a silvery flash—and with a dull *chung!* the blade snapped off at the hilt.

The Black Knight fell to his knees. A thin crack split his helm from the crest to the forehead.

However, D slumped forward at the same time. For the blow he'd just delivered had required all the physical and mental strength he could muster.

Making its way across the wild plains, the wind fluttered D's coat. Beneath the blue sky, the two black figures were both on their knees, motionless.

One of them rose, like a black mountain. It was the Black Knight. The fresh blood dripping from his head wound sullied his armor, stained the grass, and seeped into the earth.

"Ordinarily, you'd have defeated me. However, it looks like this time victory is mine. Farewell, D!"

Both the knight's hands went behind his waist. There was no conceivable way the kneeling D would be able to guard against his next attack. The Hunter's hands were empty.

Somewhere, the Black Knight heard a voice.

An elegant half-moon shape knifed through the blue sky over D's head.

Howling, a flash of light sliced through the wind—slashing from the upper right down toward D's carotid artery. The indescribable sound of steel making contact rang out and fresh blood shot into the air. Pattering against the ground like a driving rain, the blood actually sprayed from the left arm of the Black Knight.

Forgetting to even stagger, he stood dumbstruck, looking at D.

Still down on one knee, the Vampire Hunter had a black scabbard in his left hand, while a sword jutted from his right.

Strangely enough, the words that suddenly brought the curtain down on this deadly performance came from a third person.

"Like it?" asked the stout man who'd appeared from behind a rock.

"I do," D replied.

Even though the Black Knight recognized the man at a glance as the village blacksmith, he never would've imagined that Blasko used these ruins for his purification rites.

"As promised, I got it done overnight. I had intended to be home by noon, but as I was hurrying back, I happened to see you. I sure am glad I was worried enough to come out here and find you."

From what the smith said, he must've been one of the figures who'd hidden by the side of the road as the Hunter was on his way here.

"I, the famed Blasko, have never had as much confidence in anything I've ever crafted. It could cut through a thousand suits of their armor like it was nothing. Well, go ahead and finish him off now!"

Hearing the smith's exuberant cry behind him, D got to his feet.

Though blood poured from the stump of the Black Knight's arm like a waterfall, he still stood there proudly.

"Do it," the knight said. There was strength in his voice.

"I need you to do me a favor," said D. "I'm heading back to the village now, and after that I'll go up to the castle. Tell the princess to make whatever arrangements are necessary."

Not waiting for a reply, he turned his back to the Black Knight and walked off to where he'd tethered his horse. Looking at the blacksmith, he asked, "You coming with me?"

"You bet. You think I'd hang around out here with a creepy character like him?" the blacksmith replied, running over to where he'd secured his own horse behind the rocks.

As soon as D was astride his mount, a voice from his left hand remarked, "A message for the princess, eh? That's a nice little loophole you thought of."

But D paid no attention, and the smith following him didn't even notice anything had been said.

The sun set.

In Mama Kipsch's parlor, Elena was desperately trying to get a grip on herself. Not on her fear—that had faded with the arrival of the vast blueness of twilight. What she was fighting was the surpassing joy and rapture building within her; her pleasure at discovering how brilliant the night was.

After the mark of the rose had been left on her breast, she'd naturally felt a great mental shock, but physically she'd also fallen into a terrible languor, and her body temperature was dropping by the minute. Elena had been afraid that was what it felt like to become one of the Nobility. Now the village had surrendered itself to the mastery of the darkness, and her terror had vanished.

How sweet the night was. The sound of the faint breeze seemed to sweep across the heavens, the scent of the darkness was fragrant, and the moon and twinkling stars that lit the night she'd so often prayed would pass quickly were so beautiful they made her tremble. More than anything, there was the vitality that flooded every inch of her being. But it was Elena's human sense of reason that resisted this. The same blood as the Nobility was coursing through her veins.

This isn't good, she thought.

And in this manner, Elena's solitary battle began at dusk.

A short time earlier, Mama Kipsch had gone out to see to an urgent patient on the edge of the village. The first thing Elena did was lock all the doors and windows in the house, and then she went and found two items in the back room—a massive crossbow and some rope. Heading back to the parlor, she moved a low cabinet in front of the door, secured the crossbow to the top of it with some of the rope, and then used the rest of it to tie herself to a chair. Obviously she took great care as she did this. Once she'd fastened the rope to the crossbow's trigger, she placed heavy urns and books around the weapon and set it so that if she were to pull on both arms, the crossbow would put a quarrel right through her heart. Knotting the rope around her wrists with her teeth, Elena then felt more at ease.

Before leaving, Mama Kipsch had told the girl she'd be home before midnight. All she had to do was hold out until then against the sweet temptation.

And it was just after sunset that she learned exactly how sweet that could be. What a feeling of supreme bliss! How light she felt, in both body and soul! Of all the people sleeping there beyond her window, had any of them ever felt such rapture?

Those stupid little—, Elena thought before suddenly growing horrified. Was that how a Noble's mind worked?

And there was one more thing she felt. The second Elena realized what that urge was, she decided she had to die. There was no hesitation as she pulled back with her hands. And with her pull came the sound of the springs letting loose. The string groaned out a *thrum!* The bolt whistled through the air, and its tip sank into her chest on impact.

Elena opened her eyes a crack. The bolt was buried deep in her. Apparently it'd hit a bit below the heart instead. It seemed her aim was off when she'd first set it.

Oh, if only D or Mama Kipsch was here, she thought.

Bringing the knot that bound her hands up to her mouth, the girl then realized there was a much easier way to do this. As she let the strength surge into her wrists, the ropes burst free. After that, she had only to put some strength into the rest of her body. The door to the parlor opened easily. One swipe of her hand was enough to send the cabinet and other furniture sailing clear to the other side of the room.

The second Elena stepped out the front door, a pleasurable sensation she couldn't recall ever before experiencing seeped into the marrow of her bones, making her squat down right then and there.

"What's wrong?" someone asked her, although she couldn't tell when he'd put his hand on her shoulder.

"Just go. It's nothing," the girl replied.

"Well, I'll be! Is that you, Elena?" the man spat. He was none other than Gary, the guard from the tent. "Well, we don't have any obligation to help the embarrassment of the whole village. You can lie there in pain for all we care!"

The other man on patrol with him guffawed and then Gary started to walk away.

Something wet flew right by Elena's face. Spit.

Elena smiled.

What fools! How dare they mock me now. I'll have to punish them.

As the girl rose smoothly to her feet, the smile she wore was more liberated than any her fellow villagers had ever seen on her face.

Pursuing the torch-lit figures some forty or fifty feet ahead of her, Elena raced down the street without making a sound. Her movements were so effortless that it was more like skating. Her arms and legs moved with the merest thought, and it didn't really feel like they were working at all. She could run a hundred miles or even a thousand at full speed.

When she was just ten feet away from them, the two men turned. A shocked expression on his face, Gary leveled his rifle and pulled the trigger. His actions were not only reckless but also patently illegal. He hadn't so much as cautioned her to freeze.

A heated lump ripped into the girl's solar plexus, but the sensation passed quickly. Euphoria engulfed Elena.

I can kill, she thought. *I could kill this bastard. I'm stronger than he is.*

As Elena reached for Gary's throat, he batted her hand away with the barrel of his rifle. There was no pain at all from the blow for her and she didn't feel the shock of the impact, but the man still tottered from it. Swinging the gun around, he slammed the stock into the girl's temple. To her, it felt like a kiss from the wind.

Not seeming to mind in the least, Elena stuck to her original intent, grabbing Gary's throat with one hand while the other locked onto his left shoulder. Her fingers sank into him as smoothly as if she were wringing a sponge. Some part of her mind screamed at her that this was wrong.

Driven by an outdated urge she no longer comprehended, Elena shoved Gary aside. His body sailed a good thirty feet through the air, a fair amount of his clothes and the flesh on his back then being scraped off as he skidded across the ground and blacked out.

The other man had been stock still as he watched this atrocity, but when he realized Elena's attention had turned to him, he snapped back to his senses.

From various parts of the village, a crazy mix of shouting and footsteps could be heard.

Elena stepped forward. The other desire she'd felt earlier came into play. For an instant, she wondered what kind of look she must've had on her face.

"Keep away from me!" the man shouted, forgetting to reach for the gun on his hip.

No matter where I split him open, there'll be blood, Elena thought to herself.

The man crossed his arms in front of his face, making an "x."

Undeterred, Elena grabbed hold of his shoulders.

"Don't!" the man cried as his upper body thrashed violently.

The "x" became a cross.

An awful shock seared through every nerve in Elena's body. Although she didn't cry out, she writhed as she tried to fight the pain.

"The shot came from this way."

"Hey! There's somebody over there!"

The approaching voices sounded familiar to the girl.

The weighted end of the chain flew from Elena's right hand to wrap around the lightning rod on the roof of a house, and then her body swung easily into the air. Just as she was disappearing over the roof, she muttered, "D."

Needless to say, there was no one up there to hear his name fall from her lips.

III

When D came back, he was met by hostility-filled glares from the people who'd gathered at the entrance to the village, and by a despondent-looking Mama Kipsch.

"You didn't make it in time, D," the aged witch doctor said sadly before going on to explain the situation. She'd only returned to her home a short while earlier.

"Neither you nor Elena is to set foot in the village again," snarled the representative who'd replaced the mayor after his death at the hands of the Blue Knight. "That's what the village assembly decided. The next time you show your face around here, we'll kill you."

"Where's Elena?" D asked.

"At the manor, most likely."

To Mama Kipsch he said, "Are you coming with me?"

"No, it's my job to protect the village. Tonight I'll lock myself away in my house and pray for you and Elena," said the crone. Even with the malevolent gaze of the entire village focused on her, she was unshaken. "You be careful out there, D. May the Lord above watch over the both of you."

D gave a kick to his mount's flanks.

"D's coming!" the princess declared.

She wasn't inside. A gorgeous array of colors surrounded the princess and her companions—they were out in the rose-adorned garden.

"I just know it. Now, what should I do? Should I send tidal waves or mud slides, lightning or perhaps a dimensional tear to greet him?"

"If you think it for the best," replied a voice that seemed to seep into the very ground. It came from one of the two figures who knelt before her—the Black Knight.

"What are you saying, Sir Black Knight?" came the astonished cry of the other—the Red Knight. "Are you not the one who stated that if the Hunter was to be struck down, we should do so fairly and not besmirch the honor of the Four Knights of the Diane Rose? He's no slavering wolf out for blood money. When I could offer no resistance, he didn't slay me or even injure me. What's more, he didn't try to open the door I guarded, but rather left through the skylight. He's an extraordinary man. Under the circumstances, to do anything other than go and fight him to the bitter end would hardly manifest our respect for the princess and the Sacred Ancestor of her kind, would it? Or more than anything, our respect for the man himself."

"Dear me, but you do have a way with words. Do you mean to tell me you've suddenly gone from feelings of hostility to amity?" the princess laughed in a voice like the tinkling of a golden bell. "And what do you have to say in regard to the opinion he's expressed?"

His face still turned to the floor, the Black Knight replied, "At present, the defense of this castle and our princess is a more urgent matter than our pride. The Red Knight and White Knight together could probably best him. Nay, they must triumph. I'll clench my sword between my teeth and join them, if need be. However, having lost my other arm battling him, I have to say that my instincts tell me you must stop. Even if there's only one chance in a thousand, or even one in a million, we can't allow him to reach you, Princess. Kindly take my opinion under consideration."

"Very well. Red Knight—have at him."

"Yes, milady," the red figure jubilantly replied as he rose, while the massive black form behind him didn't move a muscle—as if some colossal, invisible hand kept him pressed against the earth.

"Next it's your turn, my Black Knight. If you're so prepared to sacrifice life and limb for my sake, go after D with your sword in your teeth as you just pledged. Oh, I jest with you," the princess said with a thin laugh.

If the Black Knight had looked up at her then, the resulting surprise might've very well left him deranged. For the smile that colored her rose-like lips was horribly kind.

"Your formidable skill not withstanding, it would be like throwing you naked to the wolves in your present state. Come," the princess told him. "I'll give you something to replace what you've lost."

D halted his horse before the suspension bridge.

In the darkness lit only by moonlight, the flame-like hue of the other rider was striking. He was on the far side of the bridge.

"I am second," the Red Knight called out as he drew a longsword. No doubt he meant that the Blue Knight had gone first. "Now I shall make you pay for both the Blue Knight and the arm you cost the Black Knight. Draw!"

He really didn't need to ask. An ice-like blade glimmered in D's right hand.

Though the Red Knight had been rendered unconscious by an agonizing blow from D in their first encounter, it was only because his orders from the princess had left him unable to defend himself. With a sword in his hands, he could be every bit as good as the Hunter. After all, hadn't the Black Knight conceded their close duel when faced with the Red Knight's draw?

And a voice that wasn't quite a voice whispered to the Hunter, "Are you gonna be okay?"

D's body hadn't yet fully recovered from the wound he'd sustained in his battle with the Black Knight.

"Hyah!" the crimson rider grunted with determination as his mount tore up the earth. At the same time, the young man in black raced forward, scattering the moonlight. Each proceeded an equal distance to the center of the bridge—and then there was an angry shower of sparks.

As if propelled by the crash of that impact, the two figures flew into the air, once more clashing their blades together before they landed in the center of the bridge. Sparks rained down on the shoulders of both men, but didn't linger long before fading. Their horses were still galloping away.

The Red Knight reached for a second sword with his right hand. Though it seemed like he might use two blades at once, he then took the new sword and drove it point-first into a floor board in front of him. Then, the knight's upper body dipped. Perhaps the same deadly drawing technique the Black Knight had feared was about to be unleashed on D. But the Hunter was beyond the reach of a sword blade.

"Die!" the knight bellowed, his cry of resolve like the sound of tearing silk or shredding steel.

The glint that surged from his scabbard was crimson. It slashed through the wind, howling as it was slammed at D.

D's response was nearly miraculous. While still unsure of the true nature of his foe's technique, he had his blade held out in front of himself. It was true warrior instinct. Something struck his blade, flying off to either side of it, and a heartbeat later, the suspension bridge tilted wildly in D's direction. The support wires to either side of him had been severed neatly, as if they were so much cheese.

Regaining his balance by merely shifting one leg, D said, "So it's sound, is it?"

He'd seen through his opponent's attack.

The secret of the Red Knight's unseen sword was that it was actually the sound of his sword slicing through the wind. His technique involved changing that sound into a supersonic wave far beyond the audible range—a wave that could even slice through steel.

His blade went back. Before it could send a second supersonic blast out, D charged the knight. Though not quite generating supersonic waves, the Hunter's sword did whistle through the air with an equally impressive sound.

As the Red Knight barely managed to meet the blow, he felt numbness shoot from his wrist all the way to his shoulder, leaving him no choice but to back away.

D besieged him with a merciless chain of attacks—angry blows against his high guard, thrusts at midlevel that came like machine-gun fire, sweeps that shot up from below like veritable springs. And every one of them was a work of beauty executed with perfect form, while on the receiving end, the Red Knight's own stances were all being foiled.

"Damnation!" the Red Knight snarled, making a giant leap to the rear.

As he was resheathing his sword in midair, he saw D right in front of him. And the Red Knight realized that D's blade was coming down at him far faster than he could ever draw.

"Remarkable!" the knight shouted as black steel split the top of his head in two.

Still with one hand reaching for his weapon's hilt, the Red Knight sent up a gory mist as he fell on the bridge. But once more there was a flash of light in his hand. The sound of a slash through the wind was heard at the center of the bridge, and bright blood spouted from the Hunter's left wrist.

D immediately scooped up the hand he'd lost.

The Red Knight lay motionless, having breathed his last.

A human face surfaced in the palm of the hand and said, "The lousy bastard banked the sound off that other sword."

The blade the Red Knight had driven into the bridge solely for that purpose quivered forlornly in the moonlight.

"And it's a hell of a cut he gave you. It's not like a sword—reattaching your hand won't be easy. Watch yourself!" A pained expression crossed the little face, and then it sank once more back into the hand.

Putting the severed limb into one of his pockets, D unfastened the scarf around his neck and used it to bind his wounded wrist. Then, wearing an expression like nothing had happened, he headed over to where his cyborg horse was waiting on the far side of the bridge. The combatants' respective mounts had crossed paths on the bridge, each continuing on to the other side.

Once D was in the saddle again, he turned and looked back before riding off.

The Red Knight's horse stood by its fallen master, nuzzling his now-still form. He must've loved that steed.

Turning forward again quickly, D galloped off toward his next battle.

†

"It would seem that the Red Knight has also been slain," the lovely princess remarked, her smile seeming to become all the more radiant. "Only you and the White Knight remain. I wonder if I should make use of some of my traps?"

"If it pleases you, milady," the knight replied gloomily, his face still turned toward the floor. All around him, the rose garden was in glorious bloom.

"No, I guess I won't after all," the princess said mischievously as she gazed at her loyal retainer. "After all, I did go to the trouble of replacing your arms, and there's nothing you'd like better than to do battle with the Hunter. So don't worry about me—go have at him to your heart's contentment. I'll be fine on my own."

"Princess," the Black Knight said, looking up. From his shoulders stretched new arms much thicker than the old ones. Rising to his feet, he bowed.

"Black Knight—didn't you hear? What I asked D to do, I mean."

"I should like to thank you, Princess," said the Black Knight.

"Oh, really?"

"For being so kind as to give us a chance to die as true warriors. I shall fight the Vampire Hunter till the very end."

"'As you should."

"Princess, it would seem we have lived too long here in these lands, in this castle. The day has come at last. However, I hope you shall remain well forever."

"Thank you. Well, off with you," the princess said, bringing her hand up by her face and cupping her fingers in a busy little wave good-bye.

The Black Knight seemed to smile at the childlike action.

And as the warrior walked off toward the gate, the princess watched his departure until he finally disappeared.

"It really has been a long time, hasn't it?" the princess murmured, as if she were whispering the words to someone.

The Rose Garden

CHAPTER 8

I

As D approached the steep slope, an intense air of hostility bored down on him from above. Looking up from the back of his horse, he found the Black Knight floating in above ground, seeming to carry the very moon on his back. The Hunter's eyes could also make out the wing-like flight pack the Black Knight wore on his back as clear as daylight.

"This is the end, D," the Black Knight said, the black roses that jutted from either shoulder opening their petals.

Blue darkness was born. The five-million-volt blast of electricity released by the twin discharge devices ionized the air as it assailed D and his mount. It took less than a second for the cyborg horse's electronic circuitry to go haywire–the steed fell on its side, black smoke pouring from its ears, while around it the trees began to burn just as they would've from a lightning strike.

The dazzling light had the Hunter in a merciless embrace. And in the midst of it, D grew bluer and bluer—gleaming like a radiant sculpture.

Stopping the electrical discharge, the Black Knight gasped in surprise. The brilliance that comprised this light sculpture quickly broke away from the main figure, and as the darkness grew deeper and more lustrous, the young man in black stood there serenely.

On his chest, a blue pendant quietly reflected the darkness. The Black Knight realized he'd accomplished nothing, save creating a moment of surpassing beauty.

"D, can you reach me up here?" the Black Knight shouted, his wings taking a new angle—one that sent him diving straight down at D.

Greeted with a shower of sparks as their steel met, the Black Knight easily soared back into the sky, using a sweep of his arm to stop the needles that flew at him. As he gently descended in a spot halfway up the hill, he had no weapon in his hand.

D dashed. The slope was so steep that walking itself became impossible, yet he charged up it at the same speed he'd run on perfectly level ground. Though the Hunter struck out with his longsword right as he made his bound, the Black Knight had risen just out of reach, and D's weapon instead ended up parrying two wide bands of light that flew at him from above.

"You're good," the Black Knight said, his voice coming from a massive branch on one of the many trees that edged the slope. A quick look up confirmed that the tree itself was over three hundred feet tall. "But my next blow shall be on the mark, D," he declared.

One combatant above, the other below—in terms of dynamics, the former was clearly at an advantage. D had to bring the Black Knight down to earth, yet he didn't have energy to waste on anything short of an attack that would slay his opponent.

The Black Knight left the branch. Wherever the Hunter tried to run, he could cut him down. But no, the Black Knight was convinced D would meet him head-on.

Sure enough, D kicked off the ground. One man dropping, the other rising—and the Black Knight had the edge in both strength and speed.

When D reached the peak of his leap, the Black Knight unleashed an attack. Deflecting it, the Hunter backed away quickly.

Fall!

The Black Knight was just about to issue a cry of victory when his eyes bulged in their sockets.

D remained in the air. To be precise, he was flying. His black coat had become wings that helped him hang like a gorgeous mystic bird; or a massive black bat.

Barely dodging D's sword as it came right at his face, the Black Knight was unable to do the same when the blade swung around swiftly for another blow that sank into his chest and came out through his back, draining the strength from his body.

"So, this is how it ends . . . as I expected," the Black Knight said in a bracing tone. "I'll no longer bother to ask that you spare the princess. I'm sure she wouldn't want me to do so. But it's so strange—there were a million things I wanted to ask you, and now I can't say anything."

D was slowly descending. It simply wasn't possible for him to remain airborne very long.

"It's been so long, D. What I've waited for . . . is finally . . . here . . . And I'm sure the same is no doubt true . . . for her . . . as well . . ."

Touching back to earth once more, D gazed up at the sky. As the Black Knight hung in the air, his head drooped lifelessly. Climbing the slope, D let a single needle fly from his right hand to strike the flight pack. There was the sound of a switch being thrown, and then the Black Knight began to rise. The antigravity device would probably carry the warrior right off the planet.

"Two to go," D muttered as he turned toward the manor that sprawled in the moonlight. But as the gorgeous young man sent his formidable opponent off into the heavens, his voice and his expression had maintained the same sternness that braced him for his next deadly battle.

The castle gates were open. Inside, D was surrounded by startling hues and a succulent aroma. The wind set the flowers swaying. And the roses seemed to sing,

> Go back, I say, back,
> Harm not the princess,
> For you could never kill her . . .

There was no need to search for the Noblewoman. At the entrance to the crumbling hall, D faced off against the lovely princess.

"How wonderful that you made it all this way," the princess said, shrugging her shoulders as if to throw off her amazement. The rose clenched between her vermilion lips was white. Placing the flat of one hand to her throat, the princess asked, "So, now three of them are—?" She then made a horizontal swipe across her neck.

"They met a glorious end," the Hunter replied.

"I'm glad."

"They were all worried about you," said D.

"Oh, how sweet! Although that is only natural, given they were my retainers."

"Where is Elena?"

"Dear me! This is a surprise!" the princess exclaimed. "Here I believed you to be utterly made of ice, and now you mean to tell me you're actually capable of feeling concern for someone else?"

D stepped forward.

Shrieking, the princess glided back a good thirty feet. Her scream, however, had been a tad pretentious.

"You could kill a person with will alone. Oh, this will never do," said the princess. To someone else, she called out, "Would you come out here for a moment?"

D turned in the same direction as the princess—toward the hall.

The one person he'd been looking for came out with an alluring sway. Her very image seemed to ripple like a heat shimmer thanks to the winking lights that played across her body. On Elena's chest, hands and waist jewels pulsated. The moonlight trained on her, the speed of her steps, and her delicate sway gave the gems a precious glimmer that shifted into every conceivable shape. And the garment they adorned was undoubtedly pure white silk.

"As you can see, she's fine," the princess remarked. "However, she can never return to the life she once led. For she has learned what it feels like to be a Noble."

"D . . . ," Elena said when she opened her mouth. "You came for me?"

"I have your medicine," D said, tapping his breast pocket with the stump at the end of his left arm.

"A-ha! It would appear that as worthless as my retainers were, they still put forth quite an effort. Shall I reattach it for you?" asked the princess.

"Keep your nose out of it!" said a hoarse voice.

Seeing the limb poking from D's coat pocket, the princess's eyes went wide.

"What a saucy little hand you are. Just as soon as I've slain your master, I'll give you a good thrashing," the woman said impishly. But then a silvery flash scorched through the air at her. A horizontal line ran straight across the waist of her white dress—a thread of vermilion that swelled in a matter of seconds, becoming drops of fresh blood that fell like rain.

"Now you've done it!" she exclaimed, and her cry was apparently the signal.

Bubbles formed on the surface of the blood that'd stained her dress and dripped to the floor, and then vivid colors that seemed to exist solely to catch the eye floated up into the air. Roses—four hues of roses. They formed a dazzling stream around D—and then flowed faster and faster into a whirling vortex.

Another flash of light slashed through the stream.

The cloud of roses suddenly vanished from view, and as Elena saw D standing there, she pressed her hand to her lips. In his neck, his shoulder, his chest, and his abdomen there bloomed four roses in total—one in each of the four hues.

D reeled. A terrible dizziness assailed him. Heaven and earth switched places, and even when he closed his eyes, the sensation remained.

"Every rose has its thorn. And in the case of my roses, that would be poison," the princess said with a refined laugh.

Clearly this poison was virulent enough to wreak havoc with the sense of balance of even a dhampir like D. Finally, D was forced to

rest his sword against the floor to support himself. It looked as if the very weight of the moonlight on his back was more than he could bear, driving him down on his knees.

"Before I deliver the coup, I suppose I should slake my thirst from you."

The princess walked over to D without any sign of fear and touched the rose in the nape of his neck. Though initially blue, the blossom suddenly turned crimson. It had sucked up D's blood. Pulling the rose from him in one smooth motion, the princess then inserted it into her own carotid artery.

"Your blood is flowing into me . . . Oh . . . How sweet . . . How strong . . . I can feel it . . . filling my whole body . . . ," the lovely princess moaned, her body writhing with delight and rapture.

What a terrible feast this was.

"Oh, how well I shall feed on your blood—once I've taken your head off."

The princess raised her hand casually. A glistening thread from her cuff connected the tips of her pale fingers.

"This is a razor-sharp thread spun from the veins of my roses. In fact, my knights' armor was crafted from the very same substance. I had hoped to discuss travels in distant lands with you for a while, but ultimately I shall stay here. Farewell, D."

The thread swung down at the Hunter. But when it swerved off course and tore open a fifteen-foot section of stone floor, bright blood came spilling from the mouth of the princess.

Retching loudly, she cried, "My body's burning up! This blood is—D, you're—"

Surely the princess felt the tortures of hell, and her visage become that of a ghastly reaper as her eyes glimpsed the deep red shape that'd fallen at D's feet. The petals of that withering rose curled as the brown of decay spread through them.

"Apparently, even my blood can be a weapon," D remarked.

The moonlight shone down on the handsome man, burning his gorgeous silhouette onto the floor. As D approached the princess with blade in hand, there wasn't an iota of compassion on his face.

But it was just then that there was a clang like dragging chains. The body of the princess rose, and then sank into the floor an instant later. Some sort of mysterious force had destroyed the stone flooring from below, causing her to fall.

"D?!" Elena said as she ran toward him.

"Stay there," the Hunter bade her as he leapt into the hole that yawned in the ground like a jagged, fang-rimmed maw.

Before D reached the bottom of the subterranean chamber, his coat fluttered out. Having dropped more than a thousand feet straight down, the man landed on the floor without making a sound.

D knew exactly what this place was. The lachrymose, eerie aura that buffeted him from the instant he landed told him it was the White Knight's chamber—home to the last of the four knights.

D focused on one region in the darkness.

"We meet . . . again . . . And this time . . . it seems we're to battle," said the White Knight. "Slayer . . . weeps for joy. You know . . . he keeps saying . . . he wants to kill you."

Oh, and how you could hear it—the delicate metallic rasp of iron on steel in the depths of the darkness. It was the wriggling of Slayer clamoring for D's blood.

As the white-armored form emerged from the darkness, he already had his longsword in hand.

"Long . . . has it been . . . my princess," he said, his groan of a voice creeping across the ground.

He, too, had said it'd been a long time. Those long years during which the manor of the Nobility had prospered, then decayed—the length of time they had supported their enchanting princess.

"At last . . . At long last . . . I fight a true foe . . . For five hundred years . . . I have been down here . . . waiting for this day . . ."

Was the princess actually there? Or was this merely the lament of a lonely soul?

Along with the song of his blade whining from its sheath, the White Knight cried maniacally, "Die, damn you! Die! On the end of my Slayer!"

Once his tone had changed the figure in white charged forward, whipping the wind up behind him. And D in turn dashed to meet him.

Black and white crossed.

Advancing a few steps further, D then turned. The blade of the longsword was buried deep in his right side.

Had the White Knight actually let go of Slayer? Had D's blade proved ineffective?

No, the White Knight dropped roughly to his knees.

"Oh . . . At last . . . the time . . . has come . . . The rest . . . I leave to you . . . Slayer . . . ," the knight croaked, seeming to wring the very words from his throat before he fell face-down on the ground.

Due to his madness, the murderous swordsman had been locked away in this subterranean world, but his time had also come.

D took hold of Slayer and tried to pull the longsword out of his torso, but the weapon wouldn't budge an inch.

"What's this?!" a voice muttered in the Hunter's coat pocket.

D's upper body swayed—the blade of the sword had just pressed deeper into his flesh. This sword had a mind of its own, and the enchanted blade squirmed as it attempted to fulfill its tireless craving for slaughter.

"A hell of pigsticker this is . . . ," said the hoarse voice from his coat pocket. "I can't reattach myself yet, but I'll try to manage something. Okay, D?"

There was no reply. At that moment, D had caught sight of the unearthly princess standing in the depths of the darkness. As he started to walk toward her, the ground beneath his feet twisted.

Once more, roses filled his surroundings. Moonlight poured down on the courtyard. No doubt it was the very same light that had shone when every window in the manor had been illuminated and women in white dresses and men in black attire had danced here with light steps.

D gazed at the princess before him.

"I won't run any more," the princess said, sounding like a completely different person as she looked out over the wild profusion of blooms. "But I won't allow you to leave, either. If I did, it simply wouldn't be fair to the four of them."

D didn't say anything, almost as if he were watching the lovely princess undergo a transformation. "Were you looking for a chance to die?" he asked after a short time.

"Fate had caught up with the Nobility. Even I understood as much, as did my four knights. But, you see, their pride wouldn't allow them to watch the world fall into human hands. Knowing there was no place left in the world for the Nobility, realizing that their control extended only to the most worthless and remote outposts, they wanted me to live as a Noble and rule over the humans like some great empress of the darkness. What an empty existence it is to live forever, knowing all the while that your life is meaningless—as I'm sure you must understand. You, an honored descendant of our Sacred Ancestor!"

D staggered. Slayer's blade had just buried itself deeper in his flesh.

"I chose to live here with them. And so I became the princess who did nothing but love her roses, trusting my retainers to do everything necessary to support my Noble lifestyle. That was the only way I could give my four knights a purpose and the will to live. But you see, D, there's more to living than simply having life."

The four knights said they were defending the princess. However, wasn't it more a case of the sage woman protecting them?

"And then you came. I'm certain one look at you was all the four knights needed to realize they'd found an opportunity to die. I ordered them to fight. Paradoxically, you were the whole point of their lives. Whether or not they knew what was in my heart of hearts no longer matters. I will run no more. D, come and get me."

"If you wanted the four knights to fight me, then why did you use the wraith knights, too?" asked the Hunter.

"Do you think anyone would seriously believe they could've slain you? Still, I dispatched them on a mere whim, wishing to see if I could make you and the villagers sweat a bit."

There the lovely princess broke off. The next time her voice was heard, she was in midair, sailing right for the Hunter.

"It's been so long, D!"

Their silhouettes overlapped, and the blade of a sword sprouted from her pale back. Her lithe arms trembled as she wrapped them around D.

"I wanted . . . to travel . . . with you . . ."

Looking over the whispering woman's shoulder, D gazed at Elena as she approached.

"Elena—take Slayer!" the princess cried, but her words became a moan.

When the village maid came over, she'd reached for the enchanted sword in D's side and easily pulled it free, but then she'd suddenly driven the blade right through the princess's back. The way the razor-sharp Slayer slid into the Noblewoman was a fearful sight to behold. Not only did the blade impale the princess, it also went all the way through D to jut from his back.

When Elena removed Slayer from D, the Hunter had tried to pull away from the Noblewoman. But his body was immobilized, kept still as a stone by the frail arms the princess had locked around him.

D gazed at Elena.

"I'm sorry," the simple biker girl apologized in a low voice. Her eyes were invested with a dangerous determination. "The princess showed me the way—how the Nobility live, how they think. I want this manor and its traps and its treasures all for myself. And for the rest of their lives, I wanna terrorize all of those bastards in the village that treated me like shit. I wanna be a Noble."

"Do you really mean that?" asked D. Bloody foam spilled from the corners of his mouth.

"Yes. See for yourself."

Taking her hand off the enchanted blade, Elena undid the front of her top. Her breast had no rose emblem on it.

"Right after we got here, the princess took it away. Now I'm the very same Elena you met when you first got here. But you're in my way, D," Elena said, almost seeming to shout the words as she took a few steps away.

Slowly, both Slayer and the princess's body fell over. Behind them stood D. At some point his left hand had been reattached, but Elena couldn't see how the blood-smeared face that'd surfaced in its palm was exhaling pale blue flames.

"You said you wanted to be a Noble, didn't you?"

As D approached, Elena backed away from him.

"That was just . . . Spare me, D!"

I fought with you, after all. You saved me. Really, I don't know what got into me just now.

Elena saw the flash of light from D's right hand sink into her own chest. For some reason, she didn't want to look at his face.

Sheathing his sword, D looked around the courtyard.

"So, she wanted to be a Noble?" a hoarse voice said.

Without so much as glancing at the two corpses, D began to walk toward the front gate in a horribly weary way. A tiny object fell at his feet. A withered rosebud.

Now deprived of their mistress, the flowers drooped their heads as if to respectfully mark her passing, their colors fading before they fell to the ground. After D walked away, countless dead blossoms rained down on the body of Elena and the ash that was all that remained of the princess, burying them both.

A few days later, Mama Kipsch's grandson returned unexpectedly with some news about the young man who'd suddenly vanished one night after destroying the lady of the manor, as well as an explanation of how he'd come to be hired in the first place.

After making an attempt on the princess's life for killing his unrequited love, her grandson had escaped via his homemade glider until his pursuer sent him plummeting into a mountain stream. As luck would have it, he was rescued by a Vampire Hunter who happened to be passing by.

"Is that a fact? So, that's how he came to know all about our village and the knights and everything else," Mama Kipsch said, nodding thoughtfully as she looked out the window at the manor.

Her grandson was more knowledgeable about the castle's residents and the ruins on the outskirts of the village than anyone else. D hadn't told her that her grandson survived out of concern for the repercussions that might have, given the vengeance the boy's actions had brought down on the village. After the villagers were through punishing his grandmother, they probably would've tried to discover his whereabouts, too. There was still a chance they'd want to exact revenge even now. He'd probably do well to leave the village before the night was out.

"Whatever became of the young fella?" Mama Kipsch inquired.

"After he told me he'd finished the job, he immediately took off. I've never seen anything half as lonesome-looking as the sight of him riding away."

"No, I don't suppose you ever would, either."

"But he was smiling at the very end."

"Smiling?"

Nodding, her grandson pointed proudly to the base of his thick neck.

"All sign of it's gone now, but when I was little, I got one of those roses planted in me, remember? And for two or three months after that, I was in a daze until you concocted one of your secret recipes for me, Grams. Well, I can tell you now after all these years that back then, I wanted to suck everyone's blood so bad I could hardly stand it. As it happens, I told him about that as we were parting company. And then he suddenly got all serious-looking—wait, he always looked serious. At any rate, he asked me, 'Did you want to be a Noble?' I told him that was ridiculous, and I'd be damned if I was gonna drink the blood of my family and friends. And I said that even though I was just a kid at the time, I was ready to die first. And then—he actually smiled."

"You don't say?" Mama Kipsch remarked, closing her eyes. She knew exactly what sort of smile that must've been.

Her grandson continued contentedly, "I can take pride in that for the rest of my life. I was the one that put that smile on his face. I put a smile on the face of a man a thousand times tougher and ten thousand times better-looking than me!"

Postscript

A lovely princess, valiant knights to guard her, and a sinister and powerful foe bent on taking the life of the lady—I'm sure this setting from many medieval legends and fantasy tales is familiar to most of you. And this theme is just what I wanted to try my hand at this time out. Except here, everything is turned on its head. The lovely princess is a vampire. D is her sinister foe. And as for the secret ingredient—immortality.

In the famous Hammer horror film *Brides of Dracula*, the vampire Baron Meinster drags the lovely school teacher Marianne out in front of Dr. Van Helsing, whom he's already bitten, and says, "Beautiful, isn't she? What a pity such beauty must fade . . . unless we preserve it." In the masterpiece that is Universal's *Dracula*, Bela Lugosi's Count delivers a line that's quite sentimental and not at all what one would expect from a fiend: "To die, to be really dead—that must be glorious!" And near the finale of Christopher Lee's last entry in the Dracula series, *The Satanic Rites of Dracula*, the master vampire plans to destroy the world with bubonic plague bacteria, but Professor Van Helsing makes him wince when he asks, "Is this your own death-wish?" Apparently, the eternal life and youth humanity has always dreamt of isn't necessarily so cherished by the vampires who possess it.

In his short story "Hail and Farewell," Ray Bradbury paints a grim picture of the loneliness of a man who, due to his eternally youthful appearance, eventually becomes the object of suspicion and fear for those around him and must move on to a different area. However, that's only the dark side of immortality as seen by people who will surely die. Unable to escape the absolute enormity of "Death", people continue to long for life eternal, no matter how sad it may be. Given that, you can probably understand the final actions of this story's heroine, Elena. In order to escape the fear of death, religions have been born and numerous other comforting concepts created. In the west, there's Heaven. In the east, reincarnation. And although the existence of either has yet to be proved, they can't help but make me marvel at the human mind.

I have some news that might interest fans of the Vampire Hunter D books in English. The comic *Hideyuki Kikuchi's "Vampire Hunter 'D'"* is scheduled to be released by Digital Manga on November 25th 2007, with illustrations by Saiko Takaki. In addition to the English version, there will be simultaneous releases in German, Italian, and Finnish. "D" is spreading across the globe. Cheers!

Hideyuki Kikuchi
July 3, 2007
While watching *Hostel*

And now, a preview of the next book in the
Vampire Hunter D series

VAMPIRE HUNTER D

VOLUME 10

DARK NOCTURNE

Written by
Hideyuki Kikuchi

Illustrations by
Yoshitaka Amano

English translation by
Kevin Leahy

Coming in April 2008
from Dark Horse Books and Digital Manga Publishing

Serendipity in the Black Forest

I

Less than five minutes after thunder rumbled in the western sky, white streaks started to fall, noisily battering the leaves all around the traveler. Having surmised that this might happen from the look of the sky at dusk, Ry wasn't overly concerned, but rather clucked his tongue at fate. Although it was probably no more than an evening shower, he still had to do something. It was actually his good fortune that woods lay like black haze to either side of the narrow road. Before diving in, he'd listened intently, and the thunder had died out. At least he wouldn't have to worry about being struck by lightning.

Once inside the tunnel formed by the interwoven branches, the fusillade of raindrops ceased as if it no longer existed. The forest was renowned as one of the largest and most thickly wooded in the area—it took less than five minutes for the blue sky to be replaced by jet black. Getting through the forest would take an hour at the very least, and after that it would be an additional hour's walk to the village of Anise.

"Guess I'll be camping," Ry said with resignation.

This wasn't a safe woodland. The forest spirits could breathe out a greenish cloud that put travelers to sleep so the monsters might steal their still-beating hearts, and werewolves, gold-eyes, and tree-dwellers were undoubtedly watching Ry from somewhere. A cursory glance at the tree trunks around him would've revealed the marks left by their fangs and claws.

However, now that he'd settled on this course of action, Ry quickly went to work. Taking a sleeping bag and pneumatic gun from the duffel bag on his back, he then put "owl eyes" into his own eyes. A pair of thin membranes that almost completely covered his eyeballs, they served as infrared filters, allowing him to discern his surroundings even in pitch blackness. In situations where building a campfire might prove deadly, travelers found such lenses indispensable.

Though the young man had intended to eat some jerky before climbing into his sleeping bag, his eyelids were suddenly on the brink of collapsing. After pressing on with a scant three hours of sleep per night the last four or five days, it seemed he was finally paying the price. Checking that his gun was loaded and pressurized, he'd just slipped into his sleeping bag when the sandman came to claim him. Still, he remembered to at least switch on the security system connected to his sleeping bag.

No sooner had his eyes closed than the buzzer went off. Ry quickly grabbed the timepiece he wore around his neck and pulled it up for closer inspection. More than six hours had passed since he'd dropped off to sleep.

The grass was whistling. And the sound was accompanied by movement—movement from all around Ry to somewhere off deeper in the forest. A chill ran down his spine as he watched, for something was moving through the grass. The lines a number of creatures cut through the verdure were almost elegant. Then, his terror faded. And even his surprise at that melted away softly.

A faint song trembled in the air, and the voice was soft and sweet. However, it issued from the throat of a man.

That song?! Ry thought, leaping from his sleeping bag as he did so. As he walked off with only his pneumatic gun in hand, there wasn't the least bit of uncertainty in his steps. *That song,* he thought. *Those lyrics. That melody—*

These thoughts alone swirled in his brain. A red spider came to rest on his shoulder, and something slimy wrapped around his ankle. He didn't even seem to mind.

The face of his father appeared to him. He looked weak from his suffering, and he was reaching out from his bed with one hand. The young man thought he was going to tell him something. Though his father had always been a man of few words and he'd never sermonized at his son, surely he'd have at least one thought he'd like to leave the boy. But Ry soon realized he was mistaken. He saw himself reflected in his father's eyes. However, it was not him that his father saw. His dry lips trembled, his mouth yawned like a cavern, and what came from him made Ry forgot all about his father's imminent demise.

There wasn't much he could remember of the lonely funeral service or the eulogy in which the village mayor had praised the old man as a splendid cobbler. His ears still rang with that song and the one thing he'd said.

The village of Anise.

And then his father had shut both his mouth and his eyes. That was all.

The day after the funeral, Ry had set out on a journey—to Anise. The seventeen-year-old never questioned the notion that the song and the final words the old man had left this world were inseparably linked.

As he walked, he heard the sound of rain above him. Strangely enough, only his sense of time remained—little more than five minutes had passed since he'd started walking. The singing had long since faded. And yet his body moved naturally, with clear conviction.

Far off to his left he heard a horse whinny. Not halting, Ry turned his face alone. He could see through the dark of night. The horse and its rider seemed to be swathed in a color deeper than the darkness. He couldn't see the rider's face, but he wore a long coat or a cape of some kind. Ordinarily, he would've called out to the stranger immediately just to have some human companionship. But now, the thought didn't even occur to him.

Facing forward again, Ry kept walking. The rider behind him remained silent as well. After going another five or six paces, the young man became somewhat curious and turned. He didn't know exactly why.

The figure had been swallowed by the darkness. And he got the feeling that if he were to call out, he'd receive no answer, but would be devoured as well.

I must be seeing things, he thought instantly.

Only after he'd gone another ten paces did he finally see the flames. By the capering orange flares some thirty feet ahead of him, several figures were moving around. Three of them. Instinctively, Ry hid himself behind a colossal tree. Something strangely ominous seemed to be gusting at him.

One of the figures sat before the fire while the other two stood a short distance away, surveying the area. Their faces were slightly downturned—they seemed to be scrutinizing the ground. Although Ry couldn't make out the face of the seated man, the other two sported beards. One of them wore the jacket and pants of a khaki-colored uniform of some sort, while his companion was covered from the neck down by some sort of protective metal armor. Each wore a longsword on his hip.

Crouching down, the one in armor snatched something from the grass in a movement that was swifter than the eye could follow. Seeing the long black shape wriggling as the man grasped it with his right hand, Ry was horrified.

"I got one, too!" said the armored man.

"Hell, I've got three already," said the one in khaki, sticking out his left hand.

A trio of similar creatures thrashed in his fist—surely that must've been what'd slid so noisily through the grass. Judging by the color and size of them, they were undoubtedly wood snakes.

"Good eating tonight," the one in armor said, first holding out the creature, and then suddenly flinging it into the air. His right hand became a blur. While the wood snake fell as a single animal, as soon as the flames touched it, it split into three pieces that vanished into the glowing blaze.

"Don't forget these," said the uniformed one, effortlessly doing the same to several more serpents before he turned to the man who was seated.

The flames gave off a bluish smoke.

"It sure is something, I'll give you that," the one in uniform remarked. "When they hear that song of yours, everything from the little rock-eaters to mountain snakes comes right over to us. With service like that, we'll never go hungry."

"Sure as blazes is a funny song," the other one said. Shoving his right hand into the fire, he continued, "Oh, they're cooking up real nice. Hot, though! You know, no matter how we try to imitate you, we can't sing a bar. Strange, ain't it? Wish I could've heard *the real deal*, too."

Ry thought his heart might stop. By "the real deal" could he mean the same song his father had *heard*? Who'd sung it, and where? Had one of these men actually heard it, just like his father? And were they headed someplace special?

Ry turned his gaze on the last of the three. His heart began to beat once more—loudly enough to reverberate within his own skull.

The flames seemed to add to his beauty. His age couldn't have differed much from Ry's own. The glow from the fire made it impossible to tell the color of his complexion, but he

had golden hair. His closed eyes, his lips, the line of his nose—
he was so handsome that anyone who dared to declare him as
anything short of beautiful was likely to have their heart stop
cold from mortification. The other two didn't look like they
belonged with him at all.

Feeling a little angry, Ry thought there must be some sort of
mistake.

Just then, the gorgeous young man turned to him and said, "Hey,
you—come over here!"

Ry stiffened with shock.

Apparently even the rougher-looking pair had noticed him,
and they wore daunting smiles as they called to him, "Yeah,
come on out!"

"Have a bite with us!"

II

Not surprisingly, Ry hesitated. There was something dangerous
about this trio.

"You know, you ain't the first person that song's dragged over,"
said the one in uniform. "Everyone from old men and women
right down to babies just comes right on out at the sound of it.
It's a weird song, all right. Come here and have a drink with us.
We got us some mighty fine hooch."

Ry came to a decision. This was no time to stay in hiding.

When he stepped out with his pneumatic gun pointed
toward the ground, the grins of the bearded bruisers grew even
deeper.

"Well ain't you a looker! You're liable to have the she-devils
chasing after you."

"Yessir, real men were made for traveling. Well, come on over
already. It ain't like we're gonna eat you!"

"Before I do—could I ask you something?" said Ry. His voice
was a lot steadier than he thought it'd be.

"And what would that be?" the lovely young man asked, his eyes still shut.

"Where are you guys headed?"

"Hell, we got no destination at all," the man in uniform said, shrugging his shoulders before he hunched over. Quickly sticking his hand into the fire, he pulled out a chunk of wood snake. He brought the smoking meat up to his mouth, but it stopped right before his lips.

Ry got the feeling there'd been some odd change to look in the eyes of the two men as they stared at him.

"Now *this one* looks tasty!" the uniformed man said, throwing the chunk of flesh he held down at his feet. His hand came up smoothly, and he beckoned with it, saying, "Come to daddy!"

Ry saw that his eyes gave off an unsettling red light.

I've gotta get out of here! he cried to himself in his head. *This is just too dangerous. I've gotta leave, and fast!*

However, his feet were stuck to the ground. His arms wouldn't move, either. It was as if lead had been injected into his veins.

"Come on now," said the man in uniform, beckoning once more.

Behind the boy, something moved. Passing over his head, it slid down right in front of his face. What Ry saw was a trunk about as thick as a man could reach around, and it glittered a bluish green as it reflected the flames.

It couldn't be—this couldn't be what he'd hidden behind after mistaking it for a tree trunk.

"Come to me," the uniformed man said again, and then his mouth mysteriously stretched to either side. It split from ear to ear, as the saying goes. Only in his case, it went even further, opening all the way around except for about an inch at the back of his neck.

The gigantic wood snake Ry had mistaken for a tree flicked a little red tongue from its mouth. It could probably swallow the man in the uniform whole. That thought alone was what had the young traveler completely paralyzed. With a hiss, the tongue stretched out a good three feet to strike the face of the uniformed man.

Just then, the strangest thing occurred. The man's head from the mouth up—or to be more precise, from his upper lip—flipped backward sharply. The hinge connecting these two portions was a narrow section of skin at the back of his head less than an inch wide. Beyond rows of teeth in his disturbingly large jaws, there was no tongue or tonsils—there was merely a cavernous opening as wide as his neck. And the wood snake's head was swallowed by it. The serpent's head was three times as wide as the throat of the uniformed man, but it effortlessly slid into the opening. Naturally, his neck swelled tremendously—it wouldn't have been at all surprising if it'd split wide open. Ry stared in amazement at the man's belly, now swollen like a keg of beer.

Illusion, sorcery, or reality—while the young man was still trying to decide what to make of this, the snake kept being sucked into the man's bizarre mouth until only the tapered end of its tail remained, and even that promptly vanished. At the same time, the half of his head that'd gone backward flipped forward again, coming down on his jaw like the lid of a jar. From below his ear came the sound of bones snapping back together. And then the incredible man gave a slap to his great drum of a belly and let out a resounding belch. That alone would've been enough to give anyone goose bumps—ripples could clearly be seen spreading across the surface of his stomach.

"You really do pack it away," the armored man said with something like admiration.

Rubbing his stomach lovingly, the man in uniform replied, "Hell, one this big is bound to come in handy some time."

"Won't he fight with the others?"

"Not to worry. I'm always careful to keep them in separate compartments."

The man's laughter sounded like something out of a nightmare to Ry.

Before it ended, the young man with blond hair said, "You asked a strange question just now, didn't you?" His voice and his manner of speaking were those of someone Ry's age. And yet, his tone seemed to be invested with something horribly cold and mature. "The very first thing you asked wasn't our names or what we did," he continued, "but rather our destination. Why is that?"

"No reason," Ry said, taking his eyes off the boy's gorgeous countenance. If he were to gaze at it for too long, it seemed like his mind would melt into a milky haze and he'd completely lose himself. "I was just curious," he added.

"About what? Our destination? Or about that song?" the young man said, slowly getting to his feet.

Apparently there must've been some special meaning attached to the action, because his two far rougher-looking companions backed away with paled countenances.

"That's a song you can't forget once you've heard it. Those under its spell always want to go find the singer. I heard it when I was in my mother's womb, or so I've been told. When and where did you hear it?"

Ry was just about to reply that he didn't know anything about any song, but then he suddenly became aware that an intense urge to defy the handsome young man before him had been building in his gut.

"I heard it with my own ears when I was two," said Ry. "In the village of Anise."

There was silence. A silence far more terrifying than any other change could've been.

"Is that right? I guess that figures," said the blond man. "As much as I like the song, I don't intend to go looking for the singer to hear it again. It'd probably be best if we parted company with you here."

Ry finally noticed that the young man still had his eyes shut.

"I was just thinking the same thing myself. See you around."

And with that casual expression, Ry turned his back on them. From the base of his neck to his waist he was horrendously cold. The chill concentrated in the left side of his chest. It hurt. His feet moved smoothly. The pain grew worse and worse. At the last second he thought, *Here it comes . . .*

That's when it happened. Off to his right, he heard a horse whinny. The pain and the chill vanished abruptly. Ry didn't turn around. He wanted to leave as quickly as possible.

The sound of the rain had died out.

When he finally reached someplace that seemed safe, Ry had a strong suspicion he'd been saved by the rider he saw earlier.

III

Located in an eastern Frontier sector, Anise was a village bordered on all sides by rugged mountain ranges and black forests. The amount of land cultivated was barely enough to provide for the thousand villagers who lived there, but the inhabitants supplemented their income by using the waters of the Garnow River that ran along the western edge of the village to transport lumber—an activity that helped make them one of the wealthier communities in the area.

The weather controllers had almost no effect on this region, so the four seasons came and went like a goddess robed in four simple, distinct ensembles. Summer was a deep green veil that covered everything beneath the blue sky. Fall was a coat of apples and plums that swayed with sorrow-laden breezes. Winter was a white gown that hid even the school's highest spire. And now it was spring. The season when remnants of snow that feared the warmth flowed away in the clear streams, grass and flowers put forth buds, and children's feet could be heard slapping their way up and down the muddy streets.

Many people came to the village. Merchants and fortune-tellers, traveling artisans and gamblers, con men and bodyguards, drifters and criminals . . . Still, up until last spring it had always been peaceful. This year, it didn't look like that was going to be the case. There'd been a lot of travelers that day—some were just passing through, while others had various aims and would stay a while. The peaceful village accepted them all without complaint. Even though there were some the community would've done well to reject.

There were two places to stay in the village. One was a lodging house for merchants where everyone slept packed into the same room like sardines; the other was a hotel with private quarters. Ry chose the hotel. Having camped out all the way there, he still had money to spare, and he also suspected the trio might check into the merchant inn. He somewhat regretted ever having mentioned the village of Anise to them.

While the accommodations were hardly what anyone would call spectacular, the room was at least clean. It was also unpretentiously strung with high-voltage lines and various charms to ward off evil spirits and smaller monstrosities. Just as he was unpacking his baggage and considering what he should do next, a steady knock rang out and the door to his room was opened before he could even reply.

"Oh, I'm terribly sorry," said the girl.

The room seemed to brighten immediately due to her confident tone and bearing. She must've been related to the sulky old man who'd showed Ry to this room—her carefree demeanor didn't fit that of a mere employee.

"I'm Amne. I work here at the hotel. I just came by to drop off something you forgot. Well, I actually heard there was someone about my age staying here and I wanted to have a peek at you. Mind if I come in?"

Once again, she didn't bother to wait for an answer but rather strutted right in. Over her blue blouse she wore a dowdy employee jumpsuit, but like a doe, she also had an almost impudent vigor that was violently at odds with her attire.

"And just what did I forget?" Ry asked, a bit perplexed.

It wasn't as if he hadn't had any experience with girls back in his home village. To the contrary, his lithe build and sensitive nature made him quite popular compared to all the rough and tough country boys there. Still, none of the girls he'd known had been quite so forward.

"These. Put them in if you're going to be outside at night."

A pale hand opened before the boy's chest. Taking the two little rubber items from her, Ry stared down at them.

"Ear plugs?" he said.

"That's right. So don't go sticking 'em up your nose by mistake. Why? Something wrong?"

"No, it's nothing. Why do I need these things?"

"I don't rightly know," the girl replied. "It's just a custom. We all use them when we're out walking at night, too."

"Hmm."

As he intently scrutinized the little rubber plugs, Ry wondered if he should ask Amne about the song. In a sense, it was taboo for a common traveler to ask about the history or traditions of the villages he visited. Quite naturally, in cases where the area had been under the direct control of the Nobility and their servants and the villagers had been terrorized day and night, they were fanatically loath to revisit their fearful past.

Amne chuckled knowingly.

"What?"

"Actually, the story behind the ear plugs is no big secret or anything," she told him. "It all goes back to the days of the Nobility. Long, long ago, there was a great big mansion on the western mountainside."

Ry was at a loss for words.

"While they say that hundreds of Nobles lived in the mansion, one of them was a singer skilled enough to be called to the Capital to perform at the great theaters there. The story goes that upon hearing the singer's voice, not only the birds and the beasts but even the very wind and the rain would be drawn to the mansion. And I suppose you can guess what happened to the people when they went up there, can't you?"

Ry imagined the mellifluous voice drifting out in the moonlight night after night and the eyes of the young people as they intently climbed the steep mountain road toward the mansion. For all their fear, their eyes must've been ablaze with delight. And while that delight burned in them, surely there was also some sadness.

Though she sounded far off in the distance, he heard Amne say, "The people all came back pale-faced, with teeth marks on their necks. And then, at night, they'd get up out of their beds and sink their fangs into the throats of their wives and children—no, no, that's all just one big lie."

"A lie?"

"That's right. Just a tale cooked up to scare the villagers and travelers. None of them did anything. Recent research has shown as much."

"Research?" Ry said, completely thrown off balance. "They didn't do anything? We're talking about victims of the Nobility, aren't we?!"

"No, I suppose they did do a little. After all, the Nobility had got to them. But apparently it was nothing like the tall tale I just told you. Research shows all they did was sing."

Here was another mention of singing.

"A song . . ."

"Yes," said Amne. "When night came, they'd slip out of the place where they were held and begin to prowl the village streets with their hands stuck in their pockets. Like this, kinda slouched forward, while they sang a certain song."

"What kind of song was it?"

"I don't know. All of this happened fairly far back—more than two hundred years ago. And the Nobility suddenly vanished about that time. But even now rumors still remain that they're actually hiding out somewhere and are going to swoop back down on us."

"You mean to tell me no one wrote the song down?" Ry asked.

"Who'd ever do such a thing? You think we'd bother committing to paper every rotten thing the Nobility ever did to us? But now that you mention it, I heard that when rumors were going around a while back that *they* had come back, a traveling composer went into the mansion and jotted down the tune. But that's got to be a bullshit story."

Given that she was working in the service industry, the girl's use of profanity with a customer probably crossed the line. But Ry didn't even seem to notice.

"That talk about them coming back—how long ago was that?"

"Let me see . . . It'd have to be nearly twenty years, I suppose."

In addition to the wandering composer, his father must've heard the song as well.

"Is there anyone who can recite the song?" asked the young man.

"Not a soul. A long time ago, you used to be able to hear it anywhere you traveled in these parts, because all the men and women who heard it went up to the mansion. And after they came back, the villagers who hadn't been affected had no choice but to listen to them sing. However, they say it simply can't be duplicated. The tune itself is straightforward and beautiful, but you can't even hum the first couple of bars. The only people who can sing it are the ones who've heard it themselves at the mansion. And I suppose by the same token no one could jot it down, either."

Perhaps as a result of not inhaling for so long, Amne stopped here and took a few breaths.

"Are you sure it's okay telling me that?" Ry said, smiling wryly all the while.

"Sure it is! When I'm at school, no one there listens to the results of my research."

"*Your* research? You mean to tell me that was the theory *you* came up with?"

"That's right! Why, I'm even in the 'historical research society' at school. Seems like you're kind of interested, too. So, what are you here for anyway?"

"I came to hear a song, actually."

"You're pulling my leg!" the girl said, but she looked rather pleased. She must've figured he'd enjoyed her theory. "Well, not that it matters. You know," Amne continued, "it's past noon, so you should probably head out and get yourself some lunch. After that, I'll show you around the village."

"That'd be a big help, but you really don't have to. You've got a lot to do here at the hotel, don't you?"

"Not a problem," the girl replied. "At the moment, you're the only guest we've got, and the saloon downstairs doesn't get crowded until after sundown. So, where would you like to go?"

In his heart, Ry now faced a dilemma. He couldn't very well tell her he'd come to hear the Noble's song or to meet the singer. But now that he knew a Noble was involved, his interest hadn't waned in the least. To the contrary, the knowledge had only fanned the flames of his tenacity all the more.

"Well, that's a good question—that mansion's probably pretty far off, right?" he said with a calculated disinterest.

The answer came instantaneously.

"Hey, it's no problem. It's thirty minutes by wagon. After you have lunch, we'll still have time for a nice, leisurely round trip. We've even got a wagon we're not using now. Now, run along to the diner. You go out and take a right on the street—"

—And going straight for about two minutes, he found the sign for the diner. Right above it the words "liquor" and "dry goods" were written in large letters. In small towns and villages, it was typical to combine the general store, diner, and saloon into a single establishment. Although Ry thought *they* might be in there, he wound up being the only customer.

Finishing his meal of stew and bread, Ry followed the street west. The fence at the edge of the village was where he was supposed to meet Amne.

Snow still remained in a few spots along the road. Stepping into an alley he'd been told was a shortcut, Ry stopped in his tracks.

Countless gold sparkles drifted in the air—seeds of the golden snow flowers dancing on a gentle breeze. They weren't an uncommon sight in the eastern Frontier sectors. Exceptionally heat and cold resistant, the seeds could also withstand poor soil conditions and severe weather until one bright, sunny day in spring when they'd bloom into small golden flowers that delighted people's eyes.

Bathed from head to toe in their golden light and seeming to almost suck up the glow, a figure in black suddenly stood there on muddy earth not yet dry from the previous night's rain. He wore a wide-brimmed traveler's hat and a long coat, and he had an elegant longsword across his back—that was all the young man could see of him from behind. A short distance from him, a cyborg horse was toppled by the side of the road.

Ry didn't move. There was something about the figure in black that was even more dangerous than the trio he'd encountered the previous night. Suddenly, it occurred to him that the rider who'd saved him in the forest might be this very same man.

A spring breeze stroked the end of his nose, and as if that harmless sign was a declaration of war, the figure in black made a leap. Looking like darkness coalesced, the figure sent flecks of light flying everywhere.

The roof of the warehouse off to his right was ten feet high, and at the top of it there was a silvery flash. There were two simultaneous thuds, and a brief cry of pain rang out. Ry then saw something red fly off at an angle and strike the ground.

"We'll meet again!" a voice he'd heard before shouted in apparent pain from somewhere in the heavens.

Ry ran out into the middle of the road—the spell over him had broken. As he looked up, the figure in black landed right in front of him without a sound. The young traveler was once more thrown into a hopeless daze. Could a human face possibly be this beautiful? He had to wonder if he weren't perhaps still in the forest, and all of this was a dream.

"It looks like you made it out okay," said the man.

Although that was hardly what someone fresh from a deadly conflict would be expected to say, Ry seemed free from such concerns as he nodded. "Thanks for what you did last night," he said with bowed head. "That character just now—was he one of them . . . ?"

"Apparently they hold a grudge. You'd do well to watch yourself."

"I will," the young man said, adding, "Um, I'm Ry."

"Call me D," said the youth in black, brilliant bits of gold dancing all around him.

To be continued in

VAMPIRE HUNTER D
VOLUME 10
DARK NOCTURNE

available April 2008

About the Author

Hideyuki Kikuchi was born in Chiba, Japan in 1949. He attended the prestigious Aoyama University and wrote his first novel *Demon City Shinjuku* in 1982. Over the past two decades, Kikuchi has authored numerous horror novels, and is one of Japan's leading horror masters, writing novels in the tradition of occidental horror authors like Fritz Leiber, Robert Bloch, H. P. Lovecraft, and Stephen King. As of 2004, there are seventeen novels in his hugely popular ongoing Vampire Hunter D series. Many live action and anime movies of the 1980s and 1990s have been based on Kikuchi's novels.

About the Illustrator

Yoshitaka Amano was born in Shizuoka, Japan. He is well known as a manga and anime artist and is the famed designer for the Final Fantasy game series. Amano took part in designing characters for many of Tatsunoko Productions' greatest cartoons, including *Gatchaman* (released in the U.S. as *G-Force* and *Battle of the Planets*). Amano became a freelancer at the age of thirty and has collaborated with numerous writers, creating nearly twenty illustrated books that have sold millions of copies. Since the late 1990s Amano has worked with several American comics publishers, including DC Comics on the illustrated Sandman novel *Sandman: The Dream Hunters* with Neil Gaiman and *Elektra and Wolverine: The Redeemer* with best-selling author Greg Rucka for Marvel Comics.

First came
the anime...

then the novels...
now the
MANGA!

HIDEYUKI KIKUCHI'S

Vampire Hunter D

In 12,090 A.D., a race of vampires called the Nobility have spawned. Humanity cowers in fear, praying for a savior to rid them of their undying nightmare. All they have to battle the danger is a different kind of danger...

Visit the Website:
www.vampire-d.com

DMP
DIGITAL MANGA
PUBLISHING

VOLUME 1 - ISBN# 978-1-56970-827-9 $12.95

www.dmpbooks.com